DOWN IN THE *DUMPSTER*

Dumpster Diva—Book One

Page M. Davis
Susan Page Davis

Scrivenings
PRESS
Quench your thirst for story.
www.ScriveningsPress.com

From Page:
For Rossignole: we're having one of our episodes!

From Susan:
To Miriam, my newest grandbaby.

"What is more, I consider everything a loss compared to the surpassing greatness of knowing Jesus Christ my Lord, for whose sake I have lost all things. I consider them rubbish, that I may gain Christ." ~Philippians 3:8, NIV

CHAPTER ONE

C assie Willis drove her truck into the senior housing complex and lined up to lift the dumpster next to the one-story community center. On a balmy day like this, she could think of a lot of things she'd rather be doing than driving a trash compactor.

A gray-haired man she recognized came out of the community center and waved at her. Cassie lifted a hand and smiled at him. She always looked forward to seeing the friends she'd made at Silver Dawn Estates, but she hoped they wouldn't sidetrack her today. Her dispatcher tended to get cranky if she got behind schedule on her route.

She pulled a lever, smoothly raising the dumpster and carrying it over the top of the cab. It tipped and dropped its contents into the back of the compacting truck with a satisfying *plop-plop*.

As she lowered the container into its place on the ground, her radio chattered. Mac, of course, checking up on her. When the dumpster once again sat solidly in place, where the complex's spry but aging residents could easily access it, she grabbed the radio's handpiece.

"Yeah, Mac?" Hastily she added, "Oh, this is 23." As if he

didn't know that. She made a face to no one. Mac insisted on proper procedure, which included giving her truck number every time she called Reuben's Rubbish Removal's headquarters.

"Where are you, Sandi?"

Cassie gritted her teeth. That was another thing she didn't like about her dispatcher, whom she'd never seen. Mac always called her "Sandi." It wasn't really Mac's fault, though. Archie Reuben, the owner of RRR, had decided when he hired her that her full name, Cassandra, was too much of a mouthful. Had he asked her if she had a nickname? No, he had not. Instead, he'd told the dispatcher to call her Sandi. She'd tried to correct Mac once, but he was pro-efficiency and extremely anti-chitchat on company time, so she gave up and answered to Sandi.

"I'm at Silver Dawn." She glanced at the dashboard clock. "And I pulled in here right on time."

"Good, but it's not the time you arrived I'm worried about. It's what time you leave that place. Make sure you don't stop and gab with those old ladies."

Cassie huffed out a breath. Some days she really wanted to give Mac a piece of her mind. But she needed this job, so she just said, "Will do. Catch you later." She clicked off and replaced the handpiece before he could say anything else and checked her mirrors before putting the truck in gear.

As she rounded the corner into the cul-de-sac, where several of her acquaintances lived, Lucy Jansen tried to flag her down from her front yard. Cassie waved back and resolutely kept going.

"Oh, Cassie! There you are." Another woman had spotted her. Nita Bradley hurried along the sidewalk, her gray curls bobbing as she tried to keep pace with the truck.

Cassie lowered the window and hit the brake. "Good morning, Nita."

"I don't suppose you could help me just for a minute, dear." Nita stopped and stood gazing up at Cassie, hugging herself as she caught her breath.

"Well ..." Cassie hated the feeling these requests gave her. The elderly folks needed some help, and if she had nothing better to do, she wouldn't mind. But she was on RRR's clock, after all. "Is it something Kieran could help you with?"

"He's mowing the lawn on the other side of the complex. It won't take but a minute. I promise."

Cassie sighed and turned off the engine, then she swung the door open and hopped down from the cab. Her golden braid slapped her between the shoulder blades as she landed.

"I was so proud of myself," Nita confided as they walked quickly back toward her bungalow. "I got up early and baked a pie for tonight's social in plenty of time to have it done and cooling when I left to open the shop."

Cassie nodded. She'd been to Nita's cozy bead shop, Bead Dazzled, a couple of times and admired the septuagenarian for having such a well-run and attractive business.

"Well, wouldn't you know it? The pie ran over." As Nita opened the front door of her little house, the piercing beep of a smoke alarm hit Cassie's ears. Nita grimaced. "I couldn't shut the fool thing off. Can you help?"

"Sure, Nita." Cassie wrinkled her nose as she dashed across the smoky kitchen. "Can I stand on this chair?"

"Certainly."

The annoying beep went on as Cassie climbed onto the kitchen chair and fumbled for the reset button on the smoke detector over the sink. The smoke was thicker near the ceiling. Suddenly the beeping stopped, and Cassie dropped her arms in relief.

"There. I think you're all set." She stepped down and set the chair back in its place at the table. "Better open some windows."

"I will. Thank you, dear. I wasn't sure what to do."

"I'm glad I could help." Cassie was also glad Nita hadn't tried to balance on the chair herself. She'd much rather shut off a smoke detector than find her friend on the floor with a broken hip.

"I need to get over to the shop, or I'd offer you a cup of tea," Nita said.

"Oh, no thanks. I've got to stay on schedule today. Take care." Cassie hurried out the door and down the sidewalk. She climbed up into her truck and drove the last few yards to where the community's second dumpster rested—at the farthest point of the cul-de-sac, near the tool shed.

Kieran Harmon approached the RRR truck on his riding lawnmower. Cassie groaned. Kieran was even worse than the old folks when it came to distractions. His father was the complex superintendent, and Kieran did maintenance around the housing complex. When she'd started picking up the trash at Silver Dawn two months ago, he'd taken a shine to her. Nearly every time she made the dumpster run here, Kieran came over and tried to convince her to go out with him. She had nothing against him personally, but he wasn't her type. His invitations to karaoke sessions and wrestling matches hadn't changed her mind.

He shut off the lawnmower and climbed awkwardly from the machine. He was a little taller than Cassie and seemed not very athletic.

"Hi, Cassie. How's the trash biz?"

The window was still open from when she'd greeted Nita, and she couldn't ignore him. "Hi, Kieran. Same old, same old."

"Need any help?" His hangdog brown eyes were a little bloodshot this morning.

"No, thanks. I can handle it just fine. It's my job."

"Right. Hey, you busy Saturday night? They've got a karaoke championship going on at the Blue—"

"Yeah, I'm busy that night. Sorry."

"Oh. Sure. I'm ... I'm going to enter."

She forced a smile. "That's great. I wish you success." If the whistling Kieran did while raking leaves or puttying windows was any indication, his competitors had nothing to fear.

Her radio crackled and she grabbed it, uncharacteristically thankful for the interruption.

"Twenty-three."

"Sandi?"

She closed her eyes for an instant. A gentle spirit was what she needed. "Yeah, Mac?"

"Are you still at Silver Dawn?"

"Uh, yeah, but I'm just about to leave."

"You're five minutes behind schedule. What happened?"

"Look, if I take time to explain, it will be six minutes. I'll talk to you later."

She ended the call feeling guilty and reached for the gearshift.

Kieran shoved his hands into the pockets of his blue-white-and-black camouflage pants, obviously intending to stand rooted to the spot and watch her dump the container of trash. Several other people—residents of the community—had gathered a little farther down the sidewalk and were watching too. They must be hard up for entertainment around here. She smiled to herself. Maybe she'd advise Kieran to invite the senior crowd to cheer him on at the karaoke contest.

Cassie lined up the forklift apparatus on the front of the truck and locked the container on, then pulled the lever to lift and dump it. She waited while it rose and passed over the cab. *Plop-plop-plop.*

"Hey!" Kieran's mouth hung open as he pointed wildly upward.

"What?" Cassie yelled.

"Shut it off! Shut it off!"

Cassie scowled at him and stopped the machinery with the dumpster suspended above the cab.

"It looked like ..." His eyes bugged out as he continued to stare, his cheeks going white.

"What is it?"

"I-I think—uh—a person just fell out of the dumpster into your truck."

A flash of adrenaline made her shake. It couldn't be true. Or could it? She'd heard of homeless people sleeping in dumpsters in foul weather. But this was early June, and it hadn't rained in days.

"Kieran, are you putting me on?"

He turned toward her, his face pale. "No way. It's a—" He gulped.

In the sideview mirror, Cassie could see the knot of residents edging closer to her truck. She stuck her head out the window and called, "Anybody see anything odd when I dumped the container?"

Ed and Flossie shook their heads. Lucy called, "No, Cassie," so quickly that Cassie wondered if she was hoping Kieran would be caught pulling a prank.

She turned on Kieran. "This is a trick, isn't it?"

"No. Honest."

What if it was true and she'd started the compactor? Her throat went dry. She lowered the dumpster, returning it to its usual place on the ground, and opened her door.

"You'd better not be teasing me, because I'm already late."

"I wouldn't do that, Cassie. Not to you." The way his eyes lingered on her face made her cringe.

She turned her back to him and scaled the ladder on the side of the truck body. If she had to climb down in there, she would scalp Kieran. She hated climbing inside the compactor. Of course, she had to do it at the end of each day to hose out the truck, but if she had to do it an extra time, and with half a ton of garbage in there ...

She leaned over the edge of the opening and froze. A man lay face down, half buried in trash. His unruly blond hair splayed over a black plastic garbage bag, and his arm stuck out above his head. Cassie swallowed back nausea. Was he alive? Quickly, she climbed down and jumped into the driver's seat to lock the compactor so it couldn't start, even if anyone tried to pull the switch while she was out of the cab.

For a few seconds she shut her eyes, not wanting to move again. Her stomach roiled, and she found herself praying in panic.

All right, Lord, I could use a little of that power and confidence You promised to give me.

"Cassie? You okay?" Kieran had stepped up to her door.

"Yeah. Let me out."

He moved back, and she got out again then slowly mounted the ladder. She could feel the eyes of the elderly neighbors watching her. At the top, she looked down toward them. Hal Tinley and Gerald Rogers had joined the others. All of them stared at her. Cassie pulled in a shaky breath and went over the side.

Silver Dawn was her second stop of the day, so the truck was only about a quarter full and not too smelly yet. That came later in the day, after she'd started compacting people's leftover spaghetti and used diapers from the daycare center up the street. But dropping down into the truck next to a man who was comatose—or worse—made her feel a bit lightheaded.

What was she doing? She should have just called the dispatcher when she saw the man.

Well, she was in it now—up to her thighs in Hefty bags. Gingerly, she reached out and grasped the man's wrist beside his watchband. She didn't wait to feel for a pulse. Just the cold stiffness of the arm told her. The man from the dumpster was definitely dead.

CHAPTER
TWO

Cassie had seen a lot of strange things in dumpsters since starting work at "Triple R," as she called Reuben's Rubbish Removal, but she decided this one definitely took the cake. Her brain went through a series of attempts to handle the shock. First she had to avoid losing her morning coffee and croissant. Then she studied the corpse.

Though she couldn't see his face, Cassie noted his fair hair with no gray in it. Surely he was too young to be a resident at Silver Dawn Estates. He was dressed in faded blue jeans, a black jacket, and running shoes. Before she could pin down an estimate on his age, she noticed dark red stains on a white garbage bag near him and her brain began sending new signals.

What are you doing? The police need to investigate this, not you. You're probably messing up the crime scene.

Hastily, she made her awkward way over the garbage bags and loose refuse to the ladder and climbed back out of the truck.

"Well?" Kieran asked breathlessly.

"Um, yeah ... you were right. There's a guy—a man in there. He's dead."

"Whoa," Kieran said, apparently at a loss for further eloquence. He took a shaky step backward.

9

"I think I'd better call my dispatcher." Cassie returned to the cab of her truck trying to respond to yet more messages from her stunned mind. She reached for the radio then thought better of it. No sense letting the entire fleet of RRR drivers hear this. She took out her cell phone.

Hearing Mac's voice at the other end snapped her out of her stupor at once.

"Sandi?" Adam MacAllister asked with a touch of surprise. Usually he was the one calling *her*—and over the radio. "Have you left Silver Dawn yet?"

"Um ... no, but—"

Adam rolled his eyes. If she got behind schedule again today, Archie would blame *him,* and he'd taken the blame one time too many. "I don't want to hear it. I want you on the road five minutes ago and counting."

"Mac—"

"Look, I know people have problems. You like to help. Hey, I like to help too. But you know what? You can help on your own time. It's always the same at that place. One of the old folks sinks their hooks into you, and then the whole bunch of them walks all over you. Your trouble is, you need to learn to say no."

It sounded harsh, but it was true. Ever since Sandi started working for the company, Adam had been reduced to playing radio tag with her each time she stopped at the senior complex. It was his job to make sure the drivers kept moving. Getting in her good deeds was nice, but it seemed as if Sandi always had a mammoth excuse ready for this particular stop. Adam was convinced she procrastinated on purpose.

"Yeah, but would you—"

"No, I wouldn't." Adam knew he shouldn't cut her off, but Sandi had rubbed him the wrong way for too long. "I wasn't impressed the time Ethel needed her light bulb changed—"

"Lucy," Sandi corrected him.

"Whatever. Or the time what's-his-face shot his TV set during a cowboy movie. It's not our problem, okay?"

"What if the problem is in *our dumpster?*"

Adam sighed. "What kind of problem?"

"Like ... a body problem."

"What?"

"There's a dead guy ... in my truck, actually. But he was in the dumpster. I didn't see him and I ... I dumped the body into my truck." Her voice trailed off into a husky whisper.

"Oh, boy ... please, tell me he was dead before you dumped him."

"He was," Sandi said quickly. "He's already cold."

"You touched him?"

"I thought he might just be knocked out or something, so I checked. Please don't yell at me, Mac. I'm not having the best day." She sighed. "What should I do?"

A little unsure of the answer himself, Adam opened his bottom desk drawer and pulled out a little-used manual of the company's emergency procedures. He should have known something major was wrong when Sandi called in on the phone instead of the radio. With her track record for non-emergencies, he hadn't thought about it.

As he flipped the pages of the manual, he told her, "Well, call the police for sure. Leave your truck where it is and stay where they can find you when they show up. And don't touch anything else!"

"Okay, okay. I don't *want* to touch anything else."

Sans any suitable warning, she hung up. Adam huffed out a breath. Once again, she had not followed protocol. Nothing new there. Sure, she was under stress, but these little annoyances were just part of the big pain in the neck that made up Sandi.

As he looked over the emergency procedure leaflets, Adam thought to himself that of all the people for something like this to happen to, it *would* be Sandi. It was too ironic. She'd run out of excuses to fall behind schedule, so Providence had landed one right in her lap—well, her dumpster. Of course, it wasn't every day a Reuben's Rubbish Removal driver had to deal with a corpse. That had to be a shock. The itty-bitty guilt grew larger. He didn't want to think he might be too harsh with Sandi.

But dumpster hauling was really a man's job anyway, wasn't it? Why would any woman want to do a dirty grunt job like hauling garbage when she could be doing something more sensible like secretarial work or teaching? He knew that was a stereotype, but he liked the idea that someday when he met the right woman, she would be quiet and polite. Intelligent, of course, but not too proud.

Adam ran a hand through his hair, ashamed of his thoughts. He didn't want to be that kind of a boss, or even that type of man.

Somehow, whenever he started down this avenue of thought, Adam remembered Cassie, the new young woman at his church. He didn't know her well yet, but from what he had seen, she had all the qualities he was keeping an eye out for—poise, manners, godliness.

Cassie was talented too. Someone had discovered that she played the piano, and Pastor Nickerson had already asked her to play an offertory. Adam wished she could have kept playing— the music seemed to pour out of her fingers and not from the piano.

He told himself to focus. He had some red tape to deal with. And maybe some yellow crime scene tape.

Living in town had conditioned Cassie to the wail of sirens, but now the morning air seemed much too silent without one. How long would it take the Knottsville Police to arrive? It wouldn't be so bad if Kieran weren't the only one to talk to. Or rather, listen to.

Looking past her truck, she saw the Silver Dawn residents bunched together, whispering. The knot of senior citizens, as a unit, moved a step closer.

"You okay, Cassie?" called Gerald, the retired music teacher. She recalled his saying he had tuned the piano at her church on occasion.

Not knowing what to say, she nodded and waved. She wasn't sure how much the residents had seen or heard by now. Kieran left her briefly to "inform them that there's a situation." Who knew what he would actually tell them?

At last she heard the blare that ordinarily annoyed her so much. The arrival of the police brought the rest of the senior residents outside to see what the commotion was. They formed a little crowd around the truck and dumpster, watching and calling out greetings to Cassie and conjectures to each other as the two officers began their work.

"Excuse me, folks," the younger policeman called, "you'll have to move back."

The seniors, as one, took two giant steps away, as if they were playing a backward game of *Mother, May I.*

Cassie barely heard herself talking as she explained to the older officer about finding the body. She heard the younger one using the car's radio to request backup and a medical examiner.

Kieran, though he meant to help, had the opposite effect. He energetically told his small part in the drama, of seeing the body fall and alerting Cassie. He insisted that Cassie looked as though she was in shock and should probably lie down for a while.

He leaned toward the police officer and said, in a man-to-man tone, "I could escort her to a suitable place, away from where it happened."

"I'm fine, Kieran," Cassie snapped. "I'm not going to faint or anything."

Kieran clamped his mouth shut and edged away.

In the huddle of onlookers, one of the residents raised

clasped hands behind Kieran as if to say, "Rah, Cassie! You tell him." It was Nita, the bead shop owner. So, the discovery of the body had kept her from rushing off to open her shop. Cassie felt a twinge of guilt, as if it was somehow her fault.

She shifted her gaze to the young policeman, who eyed her uncertainly.

"Really," she said. "I'm fine."

"Good. Then let me get your contact information in case we need to reach you later."

Cassie gave him her name, address, and cell phone number. She hoped Kieran wasn't taking notes.

A plain, dark sedan with a huge radio antenna pulled up, and a man wearing a suit got out. The older police officer walked toward him with a tense smile. "Detective Mitchell."

"You going to handle this?"

"That's right."

An SUV rolled into the driveway and came to a stop beside the detective's car. A gray-haired man emerged, carrying a black leather carryall.

"And here's the doc," Mitchell said.

Cassie sucked in a breath. This was getting a little too real. Detectives, medical examiner. The hearse would be next.

Sure enough, Kieran sidled up to her and nudged her with his elbow. "Look, here comes the undertaker."

The white-haired doctor stood near the side of Cassie's truck, eyeing the little ladder on the side and shaking his head.

"Nope. I'm not climbing inside any garbage truck."

"Oh, come on, Doctor," the detective said with a charming smile. "It won't take you long."

"Nope. Bring him out, and I'll make my preliminary exam here. I'm not getting in that compactor. Period."

Cassie lifted her hand, about to step in and explain that she'd locked the compactor mechanism in the off position, but Detective Mitchell had already given in.

"All right, if you say so." Mitchell swung around and locked eyes with the driver of the hearse, who was just climbing out of his conspicuous vehicle. "You. Can you get the victim out of the back of this truck if these two officers help you?" He pointed to the uniformed patrolmen.

The man from the funeral home nodded uncertainly. "I have a stretcher if we need it, and a body bag."

Cassie edged farther away. She didn't want to witness the removal. She'd rather try to blend in with the flock of oldsters and listen to their chatter.

Unfortunately, Kieran moved with her.

"You sure you don't want to sit, at least?" Kieran asked. "You probably shouldn't watch them moving him."

"I'm fine." Cassie clenched her teeth. It galled her that he'd zeroed in on her feelings when she didn't want to admit them.

Kieran gasped. "Oh, man ..."

"What?" She whirled and looked back toward the truck, where the officers were lowering the dead man to the ground.

"I think that's ..." Kieran licked his lips. "It looks like this guy I knew ... Jeff. He went to my school."

"Oh." Cassie swallowed hard. She hadn't considered that someone in the housing complex might actually know the man. "Maybe you should tell the police that. They'll want to know who he is."

Kieran hesitated, running a hand through his prematurely thinning hair. Ordinarily eager to follow any of her suggestions, he hung back, staring as the detective searched the dead man's pockets. The doctor knelt beside the corpse and checked for a pulse.

"Right," Kieran said at last. He made his way toward the detective, who had retrieved a wallet and a few other small items from the victim's clothing.

Cassie stayed where she was, and the elderly people closed in around her, murmuring sympathetic comments, but mostly watching in rapt silence.

In a surprisingly few minutes, the doctor allowed the funeral director to load the body into the hearse and take it away. The two patrol officers taped off the area surrounding the dumpster. Cassie wondered if she could get away now. Her part was over, wasn't it?

"Excuse me, Officer," she said to one of the blue-uniformed men. "Is it okay if I move my truck now? I need to go back to work. You don't need me for anything else, do you?"

"We need to empty your truck so we can check through the contents," the policeman said. "Then you can be on your way, if you're feeling all right."

Shooting Kieran a dirty look he didn't see, Cassie said, "Yeah, I feel okay. Good thing I haven't made many stops yet—you'd have a lot more to go through."

Another car arrived, and three people got out and donned white sterile outerwear, booties, gloves, and hoods. Crime scene investigators, Mitchell told her. She supposed they were going to look for a weapon in amongst the trash.

While Cassie stood by and waited for the truck to be emptied, the senior residents oozed forward and again surrounded her, offering their comfort and theories.

"Poor dear," Nita said, squeezing her shoulder.

"What exactly happened?" Gerald asked.

"Well ... I was picking up the dumpster as usual," Cassie mumbled, not sure how much she knew that they didn't. "When I dumped it into my truck, Kieran saw the ... the dead man—Jeff, or whoever—fall into my truck. I think he'd been dead a while, but I'm not sure how he died or anything. That's pretty much all I know."

"Must have been quite a shock," said Hal, a woodworker who had recently made pet caskets his specialty. "Seems a shame to treat someone like that after they're dead too ... dumped in a bin and then into a truck ..."

"Oh, don't, Hal," pleaded an older woman, Flossie, as she patted Cassie's arm. "Besides, Cassie didn't do it on purpose."

"If you ask *me*," put in Lucy, a widow whom Hal obviously admired, "he didn't look like a nice sort at all ..."

Nita agreed. "I wouldn't waste too much pity on him. Probably a heroin addict."

"I'm surprised at you," said Flossie's husband, Ed. "He might have just climbed in the dumpster for a nap and died there."

The statement evoked nothing more than a shrug from Nita.

Cassie almost laughed, but the seriousness of the situation kept her silent. And she didn't mention the smears of blood she'd seen on white trash bags inside the truck.

When it was finally emptied, Detective Mitchell walked over to Cassie.

"You said you live in Knottsville. But this Reubens Rubbish Removal headquarters is in Ellsborough, right?"

"Yes. Well, on the edge of the city. It's about ten miles from here."

He nodded. "You can leave now. If we need any more information from you, we'll be in touch."

"Thanks." Cassie walked on tree stump legs to the door of the truck. She forced herself to bend her knees, climb in, and close the door. She wouldn't give Kieran the satisfaction of looking at her friends and waving. He'd assume she was waving at him.

Though she hated to, she knew she should call Mac to let him know she was back on the job.

Before reaching for her radio, she breathed quietly, "Please help me finish the day, Lord. Just get me through it."

CHAPTER
THREE

A dam sat in the next-to-last pew wishing he'd sat farther forward this Sunday. And on the other side of the church, nearer the piano.

The reason for his wistful what-ifs, when he should have been thinking about the Scripture reading he'd just heard, was the lovely young woman playing the prelude. Cassie ... Something. He had yet to discover her last name. She'd attended his church for several weeks now, maybe as long as a couple of months. He wasn't really sure when she'd first appeared with auburn-haired Jenna Sperling.

Jenna was a chatterbox and very outgoing. She also had a boyfriend, Adam was sure. She and Travis Doake had showed up together at the pre-Valentine singles potluck in the church fellowship hall, and they'd been sitting together during services ever since. Cassie usually sat on Jenna's other side now, a quiet but attractive sidekick well worthy of notice. Her blonde hair was pulled back at the sides today and cascaded over the shoulders of her blue dress. Adam remembered that her eyes were blue too. He wished he was sitting close enough to see them.

Cassie finished a hymn and rose, gathering her music. The

regular pianist, Mrs. Paulette, took her place on the piano bench as soon as Cassie slid off it. The song leader walked to the podium, and Mrs. Paulette struck the opening chords of the first congregational hymn. Adam lost sight of Cassie, but he was determined to find her after the service. It was now or never.

The church had scheduled a college drama team's performance for Friday evening. Adam had thought of asking Cassie two weeks ago, when he first learned about it, but he hadn't dared approach her. She seemed sweet-tempered and modest ... so right in every way. But what if she said no?

Today was probably the last time he'd see her before the play. If he didn't ask her now, he wouldn't have a chance. He didn't have her phone number, and he didn't even know her last name. Of course, he could ask Jenna or the pastor. His face reddened, just from thinking about it. No, he would walk up to her right after the service and ask her.

What if she already had a date?

He refused to entertain the idea. If she said no, for whatever reason, he would smile and say ... what? "Maybe some other time." That was it. Leave things open. Let her know he'd like to see her sometime if she was at all inclined. That would be better than just accepting her refusal as final. After all, the performance was only five days away. Sometimes girls made other plans. She might be going away for the weekend, or working, or ...

He didn't even know what she did for work, or *if* she worked. She might be a student. She might be living off a trust fund and have no need to work. She might ...

All around him, people stood, and Adam jumped up, too, knocking his hymnbook to the floor. He smiled sheepishly at the older woman sitting a couple of feet away and stooped to pick it up. Time to come back to earth.

"I'll meet you at the car," Jenna said. "Travis has got to get me something out of his truck."

"Sure." Cassie watched her roommate move off down the crowded church aisle with her hand tucked firmly through Travis Doake's arm at the elbow of his city police department uniform. Too bad Travis hadn't shown up at the senior complex the other day when she'd needed help. A cop with a friendly face would have made the ordeal easier. At least the rest of her work week had gone smoothly.

She gathered her purse, Bible, bulletin, and music book, then eased out into the aisle. Travis would go on duty in an hour, so she and Jenna weren't eating lunch with him today. They'd head home in Cassie's car and open a can of soup and make sandwiches.

"Hi. Cassie, isn't it?"

She looked up and focused on a young man with shiny dark hair and very blue eyes. A little quiver of pleasure shot through her. She hadn't even realized he was here today, but now it appeared he'd stalled in the aisle, waiting for her. And he'd remembered her name.

"Yes. How are you?"

"Great. Uh ... I'm Adam. We met at the end of the Sunday school class last week."

"I remember." She couldn't help smiling. As a matter of fact, she'd remembered him several times this week, when she wasn't thinking about stiff dead bodies in her dumpster. "I ... uh ... my roommate and I were running late this morning, so we missed Sunday school."

His smile widened. "Is Jenna your roommate?"

"Yes. We're old school friends, and she offered to share her apartment with me when I moved here a couple of months ago."

"That's great." They were almost to the entry, where Pastor Nickerson stood with his wife beside him, shaking hands with parishioners. Adam spoke hurriedly, as though afraid he'd run out of time to speak to her if he didn't get it out at a hundred miles an hour. "Listen, this drama thing Friday night—are you coming?"

Cassie hesitated. Was he asking her to go with him? Maybe he was on the refreshment committee or something. "Uh ... I was thinking about it."

His worried expression cleared. "Would you go with me? I hear the team is really good."

She smiled. It would beat karaoke with Kieran any day, even if Adam turned out less than ideally compatible. Right now, her impressions of him said he was shy and strait-laced, but cute and interested in the Lord. He seemed to be a regular at both Sunday school and worship services. Jenna repeatedly advised her to keep an open mind where men were concerned. Today she would open her mind up wide and ask God to show her whether cute-shy Adam was the one for her.

The worry lines crept back onto his forehead. She was taking too long to answer.

"I'd like that, Adam."

She almost laughed as he relaxed into the winning smile again. It felt good to give him hope. She'd have to be careful with this one, though. If he was the desperate type and she ended up having to let him down ... No, she wouldn't go there. Maybe Friday night would turn out to be the date she'd waited for all these years. Twenty-five wasn't so old to be finding Mr. Right at a church function. She would find out more about Adam and keep her mind as open as the church door before them. One just never knew.

Her mom would be ecstatic—but she knew immediately that she wouldn't tell her mother about the upcoming date until after it was over. Mom tended to hover and want to know every detail about those things. Cassie didn't want to raise her expectations too high until she knew she and Adam would at least remain friends.

They reached the foyer, and she shook Mrs. Nickerson's hand.

"Good to see you again, Cassie. We enjoyed your music."

"Thank you." Cassie took a step and shook the pastor's outstretched hand.

"How've you been, Cassie?" he asked.

She gave him a scrunched-up smile. Pastor knew all about the body in the dumpster. She'd called him and asked him and Mrs. Nickerson to pray after the nightmare she'd had Friday night after finding the dead man.

"Much better, Pastor. Thank you." She hoped he wouldn't say anything direct about the incident. She didn't want to have to explain all that to Adam. He didn't belong in the world of Reuben's Rubbish Removal. In fact, she hoped they could at least make it to their date on Friday night without her having to tell him where she worked.

The pastor's wife said to Adam, "Mrs. Olson asked me if I thought you'd be willing to help with junior church next week, since her helper will be out of town. I told her I'd ask."

"Sure," Adam said without hesitation. "I'll call her this afternoon."

He shook the pastor's hand, and suddenly they were out in the bright warmth of noon. Sunny days in central New York state were not something Cassie took for granted. She'd driven the trash truck through rain and drizzle for three days this week. The June rays bathed her in contentment as she scanned the parking lot and spotted Jenna and Travis standing near her car.

"Looks like Jenna's waiting for me. Do you want to meet here Friday evening?"

"I'd be happy to pick you up at your place. If you don't mind."

He sported a mild flush, and Cassie smiled. "That's fine." She gave him the address, and they agreed on a time.

"I'll see you." Adam backed away, smiling and waving.

"Bye." She hoped he'd look where he was going before he bumped into something.

She hurried to join Jenna.

"I'll call you later," Travis said to Jenna. "See you, Cassie."

"Bye, Travis." Cassie unlocked the car doors, and she and Jenna piled in.

"So. Adam was talking to you, huh? I'm surprised. He's so quiet."

"Is he?" Cassie asked, aiming for a nonchalant air. "He's not weird or anything, is he?"

"Adam? No. He's a good guy. Just doesn't talk much."

"Well, I hope he talks Friday night. Not during the play, of course, but some. On the way, for instance."

"*What?* You're going out with him?"

Cassie turned and eyed her in dismay. "What's wrong? You said he was a good guy."

"He is. I'm just ... speechless. You haven't had a date since you moved here."

"I've been settling in."

"I wouldn't have expected Adam to ask you out. I mean, all the single gals at church have given up on him."

"Really?"

"Yeah. He's like the confirmed bachelor of Grace Community."

"Wow. I guess I'm special."

Jenna grinned at her. "I knew that anyway, but ... yeah. Adam might be perfect for you. He likes dogs way too much." She waved a hand as though dismissing that drawback. "I was thinking more of Jim Rawleigh or Gordy Herbert, but I can see you and Adam together."

"Good," Cassie said dryly, "because unless you shut your eyes Friday night, you'll see that very thing." She couldn't help wondering if she'd just made a big mistake. And yet, could a quiet man who liked dogs be all bad?

The good weather held on Monday, and Cassie decided to spend her morning off at the senior complex. She had mixed feelings about it, but she hadn't been able to stop thinking about the man in the dumpster. Who was he? Why had he been at Silver Dawn on Friday morning? If she could visit with her elderly friends on her day off, maybe they wouldn't try to stop her when she was working. And she might learn something more about the dead man.

She drove into Silver Dawn and headed up the cul-de-sac where the residents she knew best lived. She put on her turn signal at Lucy's driveway. Before she made the turn, she noticed that farther down the street several people were moving about in Ed and Flossie Simonson's yard. She rolled on down the street and parked at the curb.

Hal, Gerald, and the Simonsons stared at her as she climbed out. After a second, Gerald broke into a grin and waved.

"Hey, Cassie! Didn't recognize you without the garbage truck."

She smiled and ambled toward them. "Doing some gardening?"

"Yeah." Ed got up from his kneeling position on the walkway. "Oh, my knees! We're too old for this."

Hal was sweeping the walk, and Gerald came along behind him with a bucket of some cleaning solution and a mop. Ed and Flossie appeared to be ready to set out a border of annuals. It was a little late in the season to plant petunias and pansies, but Ed had probably gotten them for half price at the home and garden store.

"Going for a red and white border, eh?" she asked.

Flossie nodded, frowning. "I told Ed I wanted yellow and purple, but he said he had to take what they had left."

"It's okay, Flossie," Gerald said. "We'll have your yard spruced up in no time, and it will be so pretty you'll forget you ever wanted yellow."

"So, what brings you out, Cassie?" Hal asked, leaning on the broom handle.

"Just wanted to see how you all were doing."

Silence. She looked from face to face.

Cassie cleared her throat. "So, uh ... how long did it take the police to go through all that trash Friday?" She glanced toward the dumpster. "Looks like they cleaned it all up when they were done."

"They took all the trash away," Gerald said.

"Really? I wonder why."

"Cops don't need a reason." Ed's words held a bitter edge.

"They did a lot of poking around on Friday." Flossie nodded as if that was an irrefutable fact, then shot a glance at her husband. Ed just scowled.

"What's going on?" Cassie asked. "Is there something you all are not telling me?"

The four looked at each other, and then Flossie stepped toward her. "You may as well know, dear. They took Ed's .22 rifle."

"What?"

Flossie nodded, and tears glistened in her eyes. "Ed was downright upset."

"There was no need." Her husband scratched his jaw. "I need that gun for when we have varmints around here."

"Now, Ed," Gerald said, "they told you you'll get it back."

Cassie opened her mouth and then closed it again. The only reason she could think of for the police to confiscate Ed's gun—assuming he hadn't accidentally fired it in the residential complex again—would be if the man in the dumpster died of a gunshot wound. Were the cops testing Ed's varmint gun right now to see if it was the murder weapon?

"There, now, don't fuss about it." Flossie patted his hand. "You don't need that gun anymore, anyway. If we get raccoons around here, Kieran or his father will see to it."

Hal sidled up to Cassie and murmured, "I think Flossie's

relieved that they took it. Ed's not always real careful where he aims that rifle."

She nodded and said to them all, "What else did the police look at?"

"They spent a long time going over your company's dumpster," Gerald said.

"Oh, yes." Ed shoved his white hair back with one hand. "I think they might have found some blood on the outside of it."

"Oh?" Cassie walked toward the dumpster, and the four oldsters followed.

"They took some kind of sample," Ed said, pointing to the corner of the trash container. "Right there."

Cassie crouched, but she couldn't see anything other than peeling paint and rust. "I haven't seen much about it on the news. They haven't arrested anyone, have they?"

"No," Hal said. "We're watching real close. In today's paper they put a little paragraph saying they're still investigating. How long does that take, do you know?"

She shook her head. "Could take a while, I guess." Cassie never read newspapers. She got her news online or occasionally on TV. She turned back toward the houses.

Lucy Jansen came out of her driveway and met them at the end of the Simonsons' walkway. She wore kneepads over her loose blue pants. "Hello, Cassie. I didn't know you were here."

"I just came by to say hi. How are you doing?"

"Fine." Lucy held up a trowel. "Flossie said they were planting flowers this morning, so I came over to help."

"She's been asking about the investigation," Ed said.

"Oh." Lucy eyed her keenly. "There was a strange car here the other night. Friday night, wasn't it, Flossie?"

"Yes, I think so. It was parked around the corner from Lucy's house."

"But it's gone now," Lucy said quickly.

"That was nothing," Hal said.

Gerald frowned. "Maybe it was, and maybe it wasn't. What

about those rough-looking young men who came around yesterday afternoon?" He looked at Cassie. "They were poking through the dumpster."

"Do you think they were looking for clues about the murder?" Lucy asked.

"Who said it was murder?" Gerald asked, frowning at her.

"Nah," Ed said. "They were looking for scrap metal. I saw they had some on the back of the old pickup they was driving."

Hal stepped closer to Lucy. "You don't have to worry about them, Lucy. I called Mr. Harmon, and he and Kieran came out and told them to get out of here and not come back. Scavengers. But they won't be back."

Cassie smiled. She'd suspected for a couple of weeks now that Hal was sweet on Lucy. She was glad all the friends seemed to be looking out for each other and minding who came in and out of their neighborhood. Probably best to just forget about the dead man, unless the police called her.

"Heads up," Gerald said suddenly.

"Huh?" Cassie looked toward the sidewalk and saw the reason for his alert. Kieran was strolling toward them, carrying some sort of boom box.

"Well, hi there, Rubbish Goddess."

Cassie couldn't stop her upper lip from curling. "I refuse to answer to that name, Kieran."

"Yeah." Lucy put one hand on Cassie's shoulder. "If you want to talk to Miss Cassie, you'd better address her politely, sonny."

Kieran grinned. "Look here. I just got it." He patted the machine he was carrying.

"What is it?" Ed asked.

"A portable karaoke machine."

Gerald, the retired music teacher, groaned, and Cassie had a hard time not joining him.

Kieran's smile faded. "I thought maybe we could hold a talent night for the residents at the community center."

"Hey, that's not such a bad idea," Hal said. "I happen to know Lucy can sing like a warbler. And Ed, you and Flossie could do a duet, I'll betcha."

"Great!" Kieran beamed on them. "How about Friday night?"

"Sure," said Gerald.

Flossie nodded. "Why not?"

Kieran turned to Cassie. "Will you come, Cassie? I bet you can sing."

"No thanks, Kieran. I've got plans Friday night, but I appreciate the invitation. I'm sure you'll all have fun." She waved at the group in general. "Bye, folks. See you soon."

She dashed for her car before Kieran could try to pump her Friday night plans out of her.

CHAPTER FOUR

Monday's dumpster delivery routine went smoothly throughout the morning, seemingly in stark contrast to the excitement of Friday's gruesome discovery. Adam was pouring himself a mug of coffee from the morning's largely depleted pot in preparation for clocking back in after lunch when he saw a squad car pull up in Reuben's Rubbish Removal's front parking lot. After watching it for a moment, he realized that they would need to speak to his boss, who was currently covering dispatch for him. He went to his desktop computer to clock back in before knocking on Archie's office door.

"It's open," Archie called from inside.

Adam stepped inside, coffee in hand. "The police are here. I just clocked back in."

One who appreciated Adam's expedience in delivering information, Archie merely said "Okay" and got to his feet.

Adam returned to his desk as Archie greeted the two uniformed officers entering the lobby. Archie didn't invite the officers into his office, so Adam could hardly help but hear their conversation about Sandi's pickup at the senior community.

"How often does that dumpster get emptied?" one officer asked.

"That one is twice weekly, unless they call for early removal. But they haven't done that in months."

"Was anything about Friday's pickup out of the ordinary?"

"Other than the body? No."

Adam pressed his lips together to keep from smirking at Archie's obtuse response.

"How about the driver?" asked the second officer. "Is she reliable?"

If they were asking him, Adam would definitely have something to say about that, but he kept his mouth shut.

"She's relatively new, but so far, so good," Archie answered. "She clocks in on time in the morning, gives a heads-up if she'll be late, and so far I haven't had any complaints—about her, or from her. She can get a little distracted, but maybe it's just as well. If she were a get-in, get-out kind of person, we might not have found out about the body until after it got compacted."

Adam grimaced. He hadn't thought about that prospect. *Thanks, Archie.*

"Has she ever mentioned a Jeff Patterson?" the first officer asked.

"No, not that I know of," said Archie. "Of course, she's only been with us a couple of months, and we haven't talked a lot outside her interview."

Adam did not recognize the name. A glance at the officers did little to dispel his curiosity. For all he knew, they might think Sandi was a model employee, or they might think she could be involved in the unusual death. However, their visit soon concluded, which he took to mean that she was not high on their list of persons of interest.

It felt a little strange going back to work on Tuesday, and even stranger when Cassie turned her rig into Silver Dawn's little community for her second pickup of the day. She told herself it was silly to think something else would go wrong here. Once the gossip died down among the residents, she would probably hear no more about Friday's incident.

It had rained heavily in the night, and as she headed for the first dumpster, near the community center, she noticed Kieran poking with a rake near the edge of the sidewalk. Piles of litter along the edge of residents' lawns indicated that he was removing branches and other debris left by the storm.

She collected the trash from the first container and drove to where the second one sat. Her train of thought came to a screeching halt when she saw Kieran approaching, rake in hand. She had made eye contact, so there was no pretending she hadn't noticed him. Reluctantly, she rolled down her window.

"Hi, Kieran."

"Hey, Cassie! Everything's coming together for the karaoke party."

"That's good." If she kept her responses short, maybe he would take a hint and go away.

"It sure would be nice if you could come. I know everyone would like to see you there."

This sounded a bit like begging. "Like I said the other day, I've got plans." Cassie tried not to sound cold. She was relieved to see Flossie hurrying toward them. "I'm sure it will go fine without me," she said quickly before turning her attention to her elderly friend.

"Cassie." Flossie stepped up close to the truck's cab. "Can you come help me?"

She really ought to say she didn't have time, but Cassie was eager to get away from Kieran. There was a chance Flossie was even pretending to need help for just that purpose. "I can spare a minute if it's quick," she said.

Kieran scowled. "Guess I'd better get back to work. There's lots of mud and stuff in the storm drains."

After cutting the engine and making sure the compactor was

locked, Cassie hurried up the damp walk with Flossie, dodging puddles.

"I took off my ring to wash my hands," Flossie explained as they walked. "My hands weren't quite dry when I picked it up, and it slipped out of my fingers and rolled down the drain."

"Oh, no."

"It gets worse. Ed was trying to fish it out and got his fingers stuck!"

Cassie stifled a laugh. She never knew what to expect in this neighborhood. "I don't know if I can help or not, but I'll try."

Flossie led her to the bathroom, where Ed was indeed caught by his fingers in the sink drain.

"I've tried running the water," Ed told her after a sheepish greeting.

Cassie reached for the almond-scented soap pump at the back of the sink. "Let's see if this helps." She pumped a little of the pearly liquid soap around Ed's fingers and turned on a gentle stream of water.

Ed turned his wrist this way and that and tugged, but his fingers did not come loose.

With a sigh, Cassie said, "I think I'd better ask Kieran to get Mister Harmon."

"I'm too old to live this down," Ed moaned.

Flossie chuckled as Cassie made her way back to the front door.

Predictably, Kieran was loitering in the driveway. Cassie went out to him.

"What's up?" Kieran asked.

"Ed's got his fingers stuck in the bathroom drain, and Flossie's ring is probably in the trap. Could you ask your father to come help them out?"

"Oh, man. Okay, I'll get him." Kieran shouldered his rake and hurried off.

She lingered on the spot, wondering if it would be rude to just get on with her day. She was probably going to be late to her next pickup at this rate. She couldn't hear the truck's radio from where she stood, and she didn't like thinking about the prospect of having missed some alerts. She shifted from one foot to the other until she saw Bill Harmon returning with Kieran. Then she started back to the truck. Time to get back to work. She got out her phone to check the time. To her dismay, she had a missed call and a new voicemail. Both were from Mac.

"Sandi, it's Mac again. Are you still at Silver Dawn? You're not picking up the radio. Answer as soon as you get this." Adam sighed, ran a hand through his hair and took a swig of his coffee. This was getting out of hand. Once or twice, sure, but every time this one driver went to that one stop, everything got off schedule. "Enough is enough," he muttered.

He pushed his rolling chair back from the desk and went to knock on Archie's door. Once invited in, he pushed the door open and marched to Archie's desk. "Sandi's not answering my radio calls. I even tried her cell phone this time. Nothing."

Archie tilted his head up toward the corner of the ceiling and swayed his desk chair from side to side. Then he drew in a breath, met Adam's gaze, and said, "Let me know when you do hear from her. Or if you don't for another half hour."

"Okay." This seemed like progress. A half hour felt like too long a grace period, but one way or the other, the Sandi problem would be dealt with. Adam returned to his desk and did his best to focus on the rest of his drivers.

A few minutes later, the phone rang. Adam picked it up.

"Reuben's Rubbish Removal."

"Mac, it's 23. I'm sorry I missed your call …"

"Where are you?" A bit abrupt, maybe, but she had it coming.

"I'm at Silver Dawn. Something came up."

"Another body?"

"No …" she said with an irritating, exaggerated slowness.

"What else is so important that you feel you have to abandon your job to take care of it?"

After a little pause, Sandi said, "Flossie asked me to help because Ed got his fingers stuck in the sink trying to get her ring out of the drain."

"Are you the caretaker over there?"

Another pause. "Of course not."

"So, that's someone else's job."

"Yes."

Adam decided he had better step back before he really lost his temper. "Stay on the line, okay?" He put her on hold before she could answer.

After a deep breath, he went back to Archie. "Sandi's on the phone. Sounds like she doesn't have a good explanation."

"I got it," Archie said. "Thanks."

A lump ached in Cassie's throat. She knew this wasn't good. Mac had never put her on hold before. Mean as his words had seemed, he had a point. Silver Dawn didn't employ her to help their residents. They employed RRR to empty the dumpsters. Maybe she was doing something nice, but she had a duty to her employer.

"Hello, Sandi?" It was Archie's voice.

Uh-oh … the boss. "Yes. Hello, Mr. Reuben."

"You doing okay?"

"Yeah …" *Physically.*

"I'd like you to come by the office as soon as you're done with your current pickup. Can you do that?"

She swallowed hard. "Yes, sir." She'd only met the boss one other time, when she'd gone in for her job interview. He'd seemed nice, but detail oriented. And pleased to find a woman who knew how to drive a truck. Thanks to her dad, who'd taught her that skill, she got the job.

Cassie felt embarrassed as she set the second dumpster back in its place and prepared to leave the retirement center. At least no one else had approached and tried to talk to her since the mortifying phone call. She spent the drive back to RRR headquarters telling herself that if she lost this job, God would help her find another one. That was the worst-case scenario, but maybe if she promised to do better, Archie would give her another chance. After all, the body on Friday was something no one should have to deal with. Maybe he would take that into account.

Just let it work out all right, she prayed.

She realized as she parked that with Mac likely still dispatching, she would probably have to walk past him on the way to Archie's office. She'd never laid eyes on him before, just cringed when he scolded her over the radio. What a humiliating situation for the first time they saw each other in person.

She sat in the cab until she was sure she wasn't blushing or about to burst into tears. As she climbed down and crossed the parking lot, she imagined Mac as an overweight man with a mean-looking, dark unibrow. That almost made her smile. Just the thing to help her keep a straight face when she walked through the door.

Finally, she pulled the door open and strode inside. Her steps faltered. The man behind the dispatcher's desk looked just like ...

"A-Adam?"

"Cassie? What ... what are you ..." His eyes darted to the window, no doubt searching for her vehicle. When his gaze returned to hers, realization seemed to hit them both at once.

"You're Mac?"

"You're Sandi?"

CHAPTER
FIVE

A dam swallowed hard, staring at Cassie. *Lord, what do I do now?* He wanted to sink through the floor, but that wasn't happening.

This couldn't be Sandi, who gave him a headache every time he worked his shift. No, he reminded himself. *She's Cassie, and we have a date for Friday night.* As he stared at her, sweat rolled down his back. He made himself blink.

"How could this happen?"

Adam could barely hear her, but in that moment he was sure he knew exactly how she felt. Cassie was soft, sweet, and godly —the opposite of Sandi, the RRR driver.

She stepped closer. "You ... you're Adam from church, right?"

He nodded. After a few seconds of silence, he realized she expected more of a response. "Adam MacAllister. I—my friends call me Mac."

An odd look crossed her face. What was she thinking? That she must not be his friend, because he'd never told her to call him Mac?

She cleared her throat. "Well, I guess, uh, the boss wanted to see me."

"Right." He was relieved when one of the other drivers called in. "Excuse me. Archie's office is right over there." He pointed toward a closed door and turned away.

"I know."

Of course she knew. She must have been here when she interviewed for the job. Adam hadn't met her then. It probably happened on his day off. Or maybe Archie had her come in early that day, before his shift started.

Cassie walked slowly over to Archie's door and knocked softly. Archie's muffled voice gave a gruff, "Come in."

Adam said into the receiver, "Sorry, Joe, could you repeat that, please?"

Joe's question was quickly resolved, and Adam disconnected. Archie's door was still open, and he could hear Sandi—no, Cassie—talking. Her voice rose a bit defensively as she explained her actions to the boss.

"I couldn't just drive off and leave the poor man with his hand stuck. But I knew I had to keep my schedule, too, so I asked someone to fetch the manager to help them. As soon as I was sure he was coming, I got back on the road. But that's why I couldn't answer my radio for a few minutes. I wasn't out of the truck for long, really, Mr. Reuben."

"Well, Sandi, this isn't the first time you've gotten off schedule at Silver Dawn."

"No, sir. Well, I couldn't help it on Friday. I mean, I couldn't leave with a—a body—"

"I understand." A note of kindness actually crept into Archie's tone. "That wasn't your fault."

"I should hope not!"

Cassie sounded almost as if she was going to cry, and Adam squirmed.

"Well, you're going to have to make those people understand," Archie said firmly, "that you're not there as a friend. You're there as a service worker."

"Yes, sir. But if someone needs help—well—I mean, that's service too."

Archie sighed. "Get going, Sandi. And try to stay on schedule next time. Otherwise, I'm afraid I'll have to change your route and put Silver Dawn on someone else's agenda."

Adam barely heard her "Yes, sir" this time. Sandi-Cassie came dragging into the outer office, her chin drooping. She walked past his desk toward the front door without looking at him, but two steps past him, she stopped and turned slowly.

"So ... are we ..." She gulped. "Are we still on for Friday night?"

Adam stared at her. He wanted to scream, "No!" At the same time, he wanted to reassure her that everything was fine and their date would occur as planned. But ... how could he escort Sandi, the tough, sloppy driver, to the play at church? Sandi was someone he would never, ever consider asking on a date. She was insubordinate and careless and ...

He realized his mental picture of Sandi was that of a tough, homely woman who had no regard for authority. Not Cassie!

Before he could say a word, she dropped her gaze and fumbled for the doorknob.

"Wait."

Too late. She was out the door.

Cassie plodded across the parking lot to her truck feeling lower than the bottom of a trash compactor. Adam had just stared at her. No question how he felt about their erstwhile date. She'd be going alone Friday night—or, more likely, staying home to save herself embarrassment.

And she'd thought Adam was a nice guy. Mac, on the other hand, was a gritty, inflexible, and angry taskmaster.

Well, she had seven more pickups to do. Grimly, she started the engine.

All afternoon, her mind kept leaping back to the office. Not her short conversation with Archie Reuben. Her lack of a conversation with Adam MacAllister. Mac. How could she have been so wrong about a guy?

Finally her shift was over and she took her truck in for cleaning. Adam answered her call when she rang in to sign out for the day, and she gritted her teeth.

"This is 23. I just put my truck to bed, and I'm done for the day." She didn't point out that she was finished one minute before the ending time allotted for her shift.

"Roger that." Mac sounded like his usual brusque self. She was about to click off when he said, "Uh, Cassie?"

She hesitated. She was at work. No one called her Cassie at work. Should she fire back at him with "This is Sandi speaking"?

Instead, she said softly, "Yeah?"

"I, uh, I'm sorry."

She just about melted. What was she supposed to say to that? The lump in her throat was surely going to asphyxiate her.

"Okay," she managed.

"And I ... I've been praying about it, and I ..."

She waited. No way would she make this easy on him.

"I'd like to keep our date, if you still want to."

Now it was his turn to wait for an answer.

Cassie pulled in a deep breath. "I guess so. If you're sure."

"Yeah," he said, more confidently. "I just ... uh, one more thing."

"What?"

"I was wondering why you're Cassie at church and Sandi at work."

She let out a little laugh. "Why don't you ask Mr. Reuben about that? Bye." She hung up and sat looking at the radio for a long time. Finally, she made herself move.

When she arrived at the apartment, Jenna was already home from the medical office where she worked. Cassie's roommate took one look at her and said, "Rough day?"

"You said it."

"How about we order pizza tonight?" Jenna said. "My treat."

Half an hour later, over pepperoni and Diet Pepsi, Jenna said, "So, Travis and I are going to the drama event Friday. Are you and Adam still on?"

"Yeah, we are." She probably should tell Jenna that Adam was her dispatcher, but she still had mixed feelings about the situation. She wasn't sure she was glad the date had been reinstated. Once she and Adam really got to know each other, would they be able to stand each other's company? If not, how could she keep working for RRR with Mac giving her surly orders? His voice had been gentler over the radio during that last call. But would it last?

And what about the dead man in her truck? She hadn't heard any more about it, and she hadn't felt up to asking Mr. Reuben when she faced him in his office. But it puzzled her. How did that man get in the dumpster? She didn't suppose he crawled in there to die. Had someone else killed him and put him in there?

"You know what?" she said to Jenna. "I think I'm going to drive over to Silver Dawn tonight."

Jenna's perfect eyebrows shot up. "Whatever for?"

"One of the residents was having some trouble this morning. I got some help for him, but I had to hurry off and keep my schedule. I'd like to see how he and his wife are doing."

"Oh. Well, I'd offer to ride along, but Travis is coming over later."

"Don't worry about me," Cassie said. "I shouldn't be gone long." She finished her slice of pizza and rummaged in her purse for her car keys.

She brooded over her encounters with Mr. Reuben and Adam as she drove toward the senior complex. Still a couple of blocks out, she noticed a white car sitting under a tree at the side of the street. That same car was there when she passed it this morning on her way to Silver Dawn in the truck—and again on her way out. The really odd thing was that she seemed to remember it being there last Friday as well.

Cassie frowned and pulled her Focus to the curb a little beyond the stationary vehicle. She got out and walked back to the car, noting that it was a rather beat-up, two-door Honda Civic. It looked as though it had been on the road a long time. Peering through the driver's side window, she could see a keyring dangling from the ignition. Slowly, she circled the car and pulled out her cell to snap a picture of the license plate in the back.

As she ambled back to her car, she wondered why, if the Civic's owner lived on this block, he didn't pull into his garage, or at least his driveway. Why leave the car parked out on the street for several days? And why leave the keys in it? She made a mental note to mention it to Travis next time she saw him.

A woman was walking down the driveway from the house she was passing. She paused at a newspaper delivery box on the edge of her lawn and pulled out a folded paper.

"Hi," Cassie called with a smile.

The woman looked her over then gave her a pleasant look.

"Do you know whose car that is?" Cassie pointed toward the Civic.

The woman frowned. "Not really, but I saw a man park it there ... oh, it was several days ago."

"Did you know the man?"

"I'm not sure. I was inside, and I saw him pull up from the window. The fellow who got out looked like Gerald Rogers. He's a retired—"

"I know Gerald," Cassie said quickly.

"Oh. Well, I'm not positive it was him. But he walked away, toward Silver Dawn, and that car's been sitting there three or four days. My neighbor asked me yesterday if I knew whose it was." She nodded toward the brick house in front of which the Civic was parked.

"Okay. Thanks. I'll ask Gerald about it."

"I wish you would. It's an eyesore."

Cassie smiled and got into her car. She drove into the senior complex. A couple of minutes later, she climbed the porch steps of Gerald's snug unit and pushed the doorbell. He opened the door, and his bushy white eyebrows shot up.

"Cassie! Welcome. What can I do for you? It's a little late to be collecting garbage."

"Yeah, I wanted to ask you about a car that's parked out on Maple Street. It's a white Honda Civic, and it's been sitting there several days."

"Hmm." Gerald frowned. "Can't say I've noticed it, but I haven't been out much lately."

"Right." She eyed him keenly. "A lady who lives over there said she thought you parked it there a few days ago."

"Me?" He flinched, and his eyes widened. "I don't think so."

"Okay. Well, thanks, Gerald. See you around." She walked slowly down the steps and looked at the other small houses on the cul-de-sac. After a moment's thought, she headed for Ed and Flossie's cottage.

"Hey, Cassie," Flossie said with a wide grin. "Come in, girl."

Cassie went inside and turned to face her hostess. "I just wanted to check in and see how Ed was doing. Is his hand okay now?"

"He's fine." Flossie waved a hand in dismissal. "He's watching a ball game right now." The sound of the TV came from the next room. "How about a cup of tea?"

"Thanks, but I should get on home."

The TV muted, and Ed came to the door of the adjoining room. "Well, well, well, Cassie Willis. To what do we owe the honor?"

"Checking up on you, Ed," she said with a smile.

"Aha. Well, I haven't broken any rules today, that I know of."

"That's good." Cassie's gaze flicked to the bookcase beside him, where several framed photos were displayed on the top. She stepped closer. "Are these your grandchildren?"

"Those two are," Flossie said.

"Sweet." Cassie glanced at the third picture and caught her breath. "Wait. Isn't that ...?" She whirled and looked first at Ed, then Flossie.

"Who?" Flossie said.

Ed's eyes went wide. "What?"

The two of them sounded entirely too innocent.

"The guy in my dumpster," she said slowly. "Jeff something. Kieran's old schoolmate."

Ed's face turned scarlet.

Flossie stepped forward and took Cassie's hand. "I suppose everyone will know soon, anyway, dear."

She almost didn't dare, but she made herself ask, "Know what?"

"It's all right," Ed said. "The police already know."

Flossie gave a little shrug. "That's Jeff's graduation picture. He's Ed's cousin's son."

CHAPTER SIX

So, Jeff the Victim was a cousin of Ed Simonson ... actually, what was that, a first cousin once removed? Cassie was so surprised at her friends for not mentioning the connection on the day of the incident that it didn't occur to her to ask more questions. She mumbled something about being sorry for their loss and excused herself. Now she wondered just how close they had been. Whether Jeff had visited the neighborhood often. What he did for a living. *Why didn't I ask?*

Probably because she was not a callous nosy parker. After all, this was a "death in the family." You didn't go asking a bunch of questions at a time like this. Later, maybe. She grimaced at her persistent curiosity. No, she could not let this go. She certainly couldn't go home with such scant information. She needed more to go on. Time to take a leaf out of her mother's book and hover.

Lucy Jansen's front room was well-lit, and Cassie was sure the older woman would still be wide awake. She walked deliberately across the road and up to the door to ring the doorbell.

After a moment, Lucy opened her inner door and peered out

at Cassie through the screen door. Her head was ringed by a halo of curlers. "Oh, Cassie," she said, unlatching the door. "What a nice surprise. You come right in. How are you?"

Cassie couldn't help smiling at the warm welcome. "I'm doing fine, thanks. I hope I'm not interrupting anything."

"Not a thing. I was just watching something I taped." After leading the way to her sitting room, Lucy picked up her remote control and switched off the TV.

Before it went black, Cassie caught sight of the ESPN logo, which she thought was an odd choice for Lucy, who had never shown any interest in sports.

"You want anything? Tea? There's some popcorn left …" Lucy lifted a rattling paper bag from the coffee table and peeked inside. "Or I could make more."

"That's sweet, but I had dinner not long ago. I'll take a glass of water, though."

"You betcha," Lucy said. She hustled into her galley kitchen.

Cassie made herself at home on the sofa. Her eyes fell on a legal pad on the coffee table. It seemed to have a list scrawled on it in blue ink. Lucy's tight script was not very legible from a distance, which Cassie decided was just as well. She shouldn't read other people's notes without permission. Her mother had always used a similar yellow pad to balance her checkbook, and this might be personal too.

"So, what brings you here? Have you heard anything more from the police?" Lucy called.

Glad she hadn't had to bring up the subject herself, Cassie answered, "Not really. I did learn something kind of interesting, though …" She hesitated, but decided it was all right to tell Lucy. Ed had said that everyone would know soon anyway. Maybe she even knew already. "… about Jeff, the dead man."

"Oh?" Lucy returned to set the glass of water on a floral-patterned coaster in front of Cassie. She reached out to flip the top pages of the legal pad down, covering her notes with a blank yellow sheet.

"Yeah. It seems he's probably been around here before."

"Oh, then ..." Lucy sank onto the sofa beside her. "You know all about it, don't you?"

So, Lucy did know about the connection to Ed. Cassie was relieved that she wasn't spilling the secret herself. "Not all about it. I definitely have some questions I'd like answered."

The elderly woman fidgeted with the hem of her bathrobe. "It's not really *so* big a deal, is it? I mean, it isn't as if I'm deep in debt. It started out like a hobby, really. Then it was twenty dollars here, fifty dollars there. And I didn't always lose. Until lately, I was almost breaking even. Look."

Not knowing what she could be talking about, Cassie sat in stunned silence as Lucy picked up the legal pad and flipped over the first page.

"See, here's where I wrote down my picks for last month. No return on Sunday Caper—he was a bad tip—but then I had Matchless, Mosey On, and Seattle Fame. If I'd just picked Sadie May instead of Mosey On, I'd have had the trifecta, but whoever expects a filly to beat out colts for second in a stakes race?"

Cassie's brain finally seemed to click back into gear. "You're betting on horse races."

After a few seconds of silence, Lucy said, "Well, yes ... what did you think I was doing?"

"I—I don't know. I was just talking about how Jeff might have come around because he's related to Ed."

Lucy's face colored. "Oh, sugar. Please say you won't tell Hal about the horses. I think he likes me back, and I don't want him to think I'm some lowlife gambler. I never bet more than I can afford to lose."

"I won't say anything to him," Cassie said, eager to stop Lucy's babbling before she mentioned something else she hadn't meant to reveal. She reached out to the glass of water and pushed it, along with the coaster, over to Lucy's side of the table.

Lucy took the glass and chugged the water.

"For what it's worth, I think Hal likes you too."

The glass half empty, Lucy managed a little smile. "Thank you, dear. Oh, I feel so silly."

"Let's just forget about it," Cassie said. She gave Lucy's arm a pat. "You get on with your show, and I'll come back another time."

Lucy hemmed and hawed a bit and then said, "If you're sure." She glanced toward the television. "I love going to the track and watching the races in person. The horses are so beautiful and powerful! Have you ever been?"

Cassie shook her head.

"Oh, you should go sometime. It's very exciting. And when there's a close finish, oh! It's absolutely thrilling."

"I'll take your word for it," Cassie said.

Lucy was probably watching races on TV when she arrived on the doorstep. Cassie wasn't really ready to end the conversation, but she felt she should leave, so she rose. They walked awkwardly to the entry together and said good night.

Halfway down Lucy's driveway, Cassie sighed, looking up at the night sky to clear her head. She realized that she had left without getting some vital questions answered. Like, "What does horse racing have to do with the dead man?" for starters.

When she brought her gaze down to her usual eye level again, she spotted Gerald looking at her from his driveway, partially illuminated by the light from his front windows. "Oh. Gerald, I didn't see you there."

Gerald walked toward her, looking a little sheepish. "I let the cat out and noticed your car was still here ... Guess I'm a little nosy."

She smiled. "It's fine. Better a nosy neighbor than an oblivious one, I think."

"True, true. How are you doing?"

"Okay, I guess." *Why not? I'm asking everyone else awkward questions...* "So, I might as well ask: Were you aware that someone at Silver Dawn knew the man from the dumpster? Besides Kieran, I mean."

DOWN IN THE DUMPSTER

She hadn't expected a big reaction, but it was written all over Gerald's face. He was aware, all right.

"I don't know what you heard, but I never hurt him," Gerald blurted, raising a hand defensively. "I told him off one time, that's all."

Great guns. Is everyone in this neighborhood hiding something about him? Cassie tried to remain calm and not lose her wits this time. "What do you mean by 'told him off'?"

He seemed to calm a little. He stepped closer and said in a low voice, "That yahoo was dating my niece a couple of years ago—if you can call it that. Got kind of controlling, you know? Wouldn't let her have her own life, tried to get her to quit speaking to her dad. He didn't like it when she broke up with him." Gerald paused.

"I see," Cassie said, hoping he would continue.

"Yeah, so I finally called him from her phone myself. Told him he'd regret it if he didn't leave her alone. Seemed like he did after that. I never did anything. I just wanted to scare him."

"Right. I can't blame you for that."

"Does Lucy know?"

"Oh, no, we were talking about something else," she assured him.

"Good. I'd rather no one else knew about this. You know, unless they have to."

"I understand." Cassie smiled. "I won't mention it to anyone else here." She was specific because she knew she might not be able to resist telling *someone*. In fact, she was pretty sure she would spill everything to Jenna as soon as she got home.

As a medical receptionist who hoped to be an EMT one day, Jenna was not easily shocked by physical traumas. So Cassie was surprised and amused at how her roommate seemed downright excited to hear all of the details from her visit to Silver Dawn.

Jenna put on a dramatic voice. "All the gossip! The intrigue!"

Cassie giggled. "Come on, what do you think? Isn't it weird that so many of them know him? Well, were connected to him?"

"It is weird. Very weird." Jenna tapped a finger against her face for a few seconds. "Want me to call Travis?"

"No."

They fell silent until Cassie said, "Is Travis on duty tonight?"

"Yeah, but he's had a lot of downtime lately."

"Oh."

More silence. Again, Cassie broke it. "I guess you could call him. But don't tell him what I told you. Just see if he's heard anything."

"Okay." Jenna got out her phone.

"And don't tell him I said to ask."

"I won't."

Cassie bit her lip. "There's one other thing."

"What?"

"There's this white car sitting over on Maple Street near Silver Dawn's entrance. I was thinking maybe I should mention it to the police." Cassie got up and went to the counter, where she'd stashed her purse in a corner. She took out her phone and tapped it a few times. "I noticed it sitting by the curb today, and I think it's been parked there since at least Friday. I'm not sure—it could have been moved. But when I looked at it today, the keys were in the ignition. It's a Honda."

"You took pictures of it?" Jenna studied the screen.

"Yeah. I was surprised it stayed there that long, and a woman who lives over there said someone parked it there and left it—maybe Friday."

Jenna frowned. "Isn't that the day—"

"Yeah."

"Okay, I'll tell Travis. Can you send him these photos? If Trav thinks it's important, the police can trace it."

"Sure."

Cassie forced herself to keep silent during their brief exchange.

"Hey, hon. Nothing much, just wanted to know if you found out anything about Cassie's corpse."

Cassie's mouth fell open, and she mouthed, "What?"

Jenna laughed. "You know, the body in the dumpster. Oh. Hmm. Well, I'm super curious, so let me know if you hear anything. Listen, Cassie saw something near there—a car she thinks was left there on Friday."

Clenching her teeth, Cassie waited while Jenna gave Travis the details and ended the call.

"Yup, that's all. I'll have her send the pix right away. Love you too. Bye."

"*My* corpse?" Cassie demanded.

With a giggle, Jenna said, "Well, that wasn't much help. Travis said he's heard about the case, but he isn't assigned to it."

"Too bad."

"Yeah. Still, he could get pulled in if they need more help on it. You have his number, right? Send him the photos, and they'll check the license plate."

"Okay." Cassie sighed and sent the pictures. "There are too many potential suspects, you know? What with Ed, Lucy, and Gerald … Not to mention Kieran. They all knew the guy, but they didn't say anything on Friday. Well, just Kieran."

"What if they *all* did it? You know, they all had something against him, so they made a plot together and shared the guilt. There was an episode like that on *Suspect List* a couple of weeks ago."

"Jenna, any crime show that runs more than two seasons will eventually have a *Murder On the Orient Express* episode. You know that, right?"

Jenna pouted.

"Along with a *Rear Window* episode and a *Twelve Angry Men* episode …"

"All right, all right."

But Cassie wasn't as confident as she sounded. What if it wasn't such a silly idea? She silently said a prayer that Jenna was wrong and her senior friends had nothing to do with the death.

CHAPTER
SEVEN

Adam guided two dogs, a beagle and what he thought was a Labrador retriever cross, out the back door of the Humane Society shelter, into the large play yard.

"Here you go." He stooped and removed their leashes, allowing them to run free. The beagle, Smokey, took off immediately for a dash around the grassy yard, while Bingo hovered nearby, whining a little and looking up at him expectantly.

Adam knelt and ruffled the thick hair on Bingo's neck. "It's okay, fella. You can run around too." He gave the dog a firm pat on the head and stood. Bingo raced off, meeting up with Smokey near the fence and continuing to run beside him.

Volunteering with the animals was one of Adam's favorite activities. He'd been doing it every Tuesday evening for several months. Someday he hoped he could have a dog of his own, but right now the apartment building where he lived didn't allow pets. He hadn't had one before moving out on his own either, because his stepfather didn't like dogs. How different might their relationship have been if they'd had a dog to cement a bond between them?

The two dogs approached him. He grinned and dug a rubber ball from his pocket.

"Go get it, boys. Fetch!" He threw the ball into the middle of the yard and watched the dogs tear after it. Smokey reached it first and veered away from Bingo as he hurried back to Adam with the ball clutched in his teeth.

"Good boy." Adam took it and patted Smokey, then threw the ball to the side so that Bingo was nearest to its path this time.

As the dogs bolted away from him, his thoughts strayed to Cassie. Did she like dogs? What did she do when she wasn't driving a garbage truck or playing the piano? If he were honest, he was a little nervous about their planned date. She'd expected him to call it off. Would he constantly think of her as a truck driver while they were out together?

Lord, help me to see Cassie as the godly woman she really is. He would still have to treat her as a subordinate when she was on the job. But not as in inferior. Could he be nice to Sandi, the persona he worked with? He swallowed hard. *Help me to treat her with respect.*

That triggered a new thought. How did Sandi perceive him? She'd only ever talked to him over the radio until she walked into the office to report to Archie. Was he a mean, demanding supervisor? He hoped not, but he had a strong inkling that Sandi wasn't the only one who came across as less than the ideal work partner.

On Wednesday morning, a work order lay on his desk. He needed to assign one of the drivers to deliver several dumpsters to new clients. It was a plum assignment, really—much more pleasant than collecting trash. In the past, he wouldn't have given the task to Sandi. But why not? Was it because he'd have to deal with her in person to cope with the paperwork? He began to realize how unfair he'd been because he'd disliked her, when he didn't even know her.

He switched his radio to talk mode and gave Sandi's call sign.

"This is Sandi," she said.

"Hey, I've got a special assignment for you this morning, if you want it."

"Uh ... I have my east side run."

"We can swap that with one of the other drivers." Adam quickly checked his lists. "Harry can do it today."

"Okay, sure."

"Come on into the office, then. I'll give you some paperwork. You'll have to get signatures at each place you deliver to."

"I'll be right in."

Adam let out a big sigh. This would be a fairly easy day for Sandi. It was about time he gave her a break. And it felt good. Not only that, but he'd get to see Cassie for a few minutes.

He was still mixing them up in his mind. *Lord, help me to make sense of this.* When he'd asked Archie about the name confusion, his boss had shrugged.

"Isn't Sandi a nickname for Cassandra?" Archie had asked.

"Well, I guess for some people. But she goes by Cassie."

"Whatever."

Adam let it drop. Archie would probably continue to call her Sandi for as long as she worked at RRR.

When she burst through the office doorway, Adam smiled at her. "Listen, before I give you the details, is it okay if I call you Cassie at work now? Unless—"

"I'd like that," she said. "Thanks. Now, what do we have?"

On Thursday and Friday, Cassie was back on her regular schedule. Wednesday morning had been a refreshing change, but she also enjoyed the regularity of her usual runs. On Friday, her trash route again included Silver Dawn, and she honestly looked forward to seeing her friends there, although the thought that one or more of them could be involved in Jeff's death upset her. She chose to put that idea out of her mind and do her job.

When she drove into the complex and approached the first dumpster, she was surprised to see Hal sitting on his front porch. He was working on something he held in his hands, and she wondered what it was. After dumping the container's contents into her truck, she strolled over to his driveway and up to the steps.

"Hi, Hal."

"Cassie." His smile seemed genuine enough. Now she just had to remember not to mention Lucy's proclivity for the racetrack.

"What are you doing?" she asked.

"What? Oh, this?" He opened his hands, revealing a knife with a six-inch blade. "Just sharpening it." He held up a small device with his left hand, and she saw that it had a round wheel that was a sharpening stone.

She gulped. "Oh."

"It's the knife I use for cleaning fish," Hal said. "My grandson wants to take me fishing next weekend."

"So you're preparing in advance."

"Yeah, just a couple of things. I dug out my fishing vest and my hat with the feather flies on it."

"You're going fly fishing?"

"I'm not sure. I suspect we'll be out on the lake. But it's the fashion when you're angling, you know?"

Cassie managed another smile. "Sure. I'm certain you'll be stylish."

She turned away and went back to the truck. At the entrance to the complex, she paused. Ed was just pulling in off the street. He braked and rolled down his window, so she put hers down too.

"Hi, Ed," she called.

"Hey, Cassie! Good to see you."

"Where you been?" she asked.

"Over to the gun shop on Hill Street."

She blinked. "The gun shop?"

"Yeah." He rummaged on the seat, and a moment later he held out a small open case about the size of a large book. Inside it, a lethal-looking pistol nestled in a velvet lining.

"Wow."

Ed grinned. "Isn't she a beauty?"

"Wh-why did you get a gun?" Cassie asked.

"Well, you know, Flossie's been a little nervous since the, um, incident with the dumpster."

"I see." But Cassie wasn't sure she did see.

"They have a shooting range at the back of the gun shop, and I'm going to go once a week until I'm a decent shot."

"Okay. Is Flossie going to learn to shoot too?"

"I'm not sure yet. We'll see."

Cassie tried to block out a mental image of all the seniors packing heat around their complex.

"Well, I'll see ya, Ed."

He waved and drove on toward his home.

Cassie pulled out onto the street. Everything the oldsters were doing looked suspicious now. Would they really be safer with more weapons around?

Adam was about to knock on Cassie's door a second time when it opened. He looked at her face. She didn't look happy to see him. In fact, her lower lip trembled.

"Hi," he said. "Are you okay?"

"Yes. Come on in." She turned toward the sofa, where her jacket lay.

He stepped inside, shut the door, and took a deep breath. "Cassie, if you don't want to go ..."

"No," she said quickly, "I do. I mean ..." She studied him for a moment. "If you still do."

"Yes, I want to. I want to go together, that is."

She nodded, but her brow was still furrowed. "Let me just ..." She bent and retrieved her purse from the couch.

The ride to the church was quiet. After a couple of minutes, Adam ventured, "So, your run today went okay."

"Yes." She was quiet for a moment then looked over at him. "The folks at Silver Dawn are a little on edge."

"I guess that's understandable."

"Yeah."

He couldn't think of anything else to say.

They sat side by side through the play. It had a good storyline, and the actors presented it well, but he couldn't keep his mind on it. By the end of the first act, he'd decided Cassie really didn't want to be here beside him. Then she turned to him as the lights went up and gave him a weak smile.

"Everything all right?" he asked.

She nodded. "I might visit the ladies' room."

"Okay. Would you like a cup of punch?" The church ladies were serving light refreshments in the foyer.

"Uh, no, I'm okay. Thanks." She glided off toward the back of the auditorium.

A couple of church attendees stopped at the end of the row to speak to him. Adam stood and tried to respond cheerfully. He spotted Jenna and Travis sitting on the other side of the aisle and back a couple of rows. Jenna grinned and gave him a discreet wave. Her smile was ten times brighter than Cassie's.

When she returned, Cassie said apologetically, "Sorry I took so long. I ran into Pastor Nickerson, and he wanted to know if I could play next Wednesday evening. Mrs. Paulette will be away."

"Did you say yes?" He stood until she'd resumed her seat, then sank down beside her.

"Uh-huh."

The lights dimmed, and the last half of the play began.

Adam forced himself to follow along, and at one point, when Cassie laughed out loud at something the lead actress said, he decided he actually was having a good time.

When it ended, they clapped a long time with the rest of the audience. The applause quieted, and Adam stood and turned to her. She had picked up her jacket, and he took it, to help her put it on.

"Oh, thank you," she murmured.

"Listen, it's still early," Adam said. "What would you say to getting a milkshake or something? We could talk …"

He was afraid she'd make an excuse, but after a moment, she offered a smile and said softly, "I like chocolate shakes."

"Terrific." His smile stretched his cheeks. "Let's go."

Twenty minutes later, they had their order and were seated across from each other in a booth at a fast-food restaurant. They chatted about their hobbies and interests.

"I like reading, especially mystery novels," Cassie said.

"I do too. I like some of the older writers."

"Agatha Christie?" she asked.

"Well, yeah. How about Ellis Peters?"

"I love Brother Cadfael."

Adam nodded. "Have you read her series about the Felse family?"

"I have." Her face lit up, and they discussed the series for several minutes.

A lull came, and Cassie sipped her milkshake. Adam tried desperately to think of another topic.

"How about cop shows?"

"Well, I like some of them. If they're not too violent."

"Yeah."

"You know …" Cassie gazed at him, and her frown puckered her smooth forehead again.

"What?" Adam asked.

"Well, it's silly, but I kind of didn't like Mac."

He stared at her then touched his chest. "You mean me?"

"I mean my boss. My dispatcher, that is. Mac seemed ... I don't know. Between you and me, I was a little afraid of him."

"You mean me."

"No, I mean the Mac on the radio. The one who handed out assignments and growled at me if I was late getting back to Triple-R."

"I'm sorry." He pulled in a deep breath. "I confess, I wasn't very nice to 'Sandi.' And I didn't even know her. You." He shook his head. "This week, I've had to reevaluate myself as a supervisor. And I realized I may have been efficient, but I wasn't very likable to the employees. Can you forgive me?" Adam held his breath as he awaited her answer.

"Hmm. I think I could give you another chance." Her eyes brightened.

"Thank you. I don't want you or any of the other drivers to be afraid of me or to dislike me."

"Well, you have to keep the business on track."

"Yeah, but I think I can do it with a better attitude. I ..." He hesitated and then went on. "I'm asking God to help me improve my own performance. I hope that I can then help the drivers to improve theirs, instead of harping at them for their mistakes."

"Wow." She drank through her straw and set the cup down. "I like the Adam I see tonight, if that makes a difference."

"It does. A big difference. And I like Cassie—in fact, I explained about your name to Archie, and he said I can call you Cassie at work now."

She smiled. "That's progress. Thanks."

"You're welcome. I ... plan to try harder."

"I'll try too. I know I shouldn't have let my emotions cause me to be rude to you or anyone else. I admit the whole body in the dumpster thing did upset me."

"Nightmares?" Adam asked.

"No, but I keep thinking about it and wondering if I should have acted differently."

"He was dead before you got there, wasn't he?"

"Well, yes. And I know it's not my fault. But ..."

"What?"

She raised her eyes—blue-gray today like an overcast sky. "I'm a little concerned about my friends over there. The seniors."

"The police are on the job. They'll find out who killed that guy."

"I'm sure they will, but ... See, several of them knew Jeff."

Adam tried to see where she was going and couldn't quite glimpse it. "And you're not sure they're safe, or what?"

"Well, some of them don't think they're safe. Ed Simonson bought a gun today."

"Whoa."

"Yeah, and Hal Tinley was sharpening a knife when I got there." Cassie waved a hand in dismissal. "He said it was for cleaning fish."

"It probably was."

"Still." She didn't look convinced.

"You don't think any of the old folks were involved in the death, do you?"

"Well, no. They're all nice people. But I can't help wondering, you know?"

He nodded slowly. "Cassie, I know what I just said about the police. But we have to remember, too, that God is in charge."

"Yes, I know you're right, But sometimes it's hard to keep that in mind."

Adam glanced at his watch. "I should get you home."

"Yes, I should sleep. But, Adam ..."

"What?"

"I was wondering ... Would you consider ..."

He couldn't help smiling. "What is it?"

"We're both off tomorrow. Would you go to Silver Dawn with me? I want to talk to some of my friends there when I'm not on a schedule."

His immediate inner reaction was *No way!* Those people had caused him a ton of headaches and landed Cassie in trouble by messing up her schedule several times.

But she was asking for his help. If he turned her down, what would that do to their fragile relationship?

He stood and reached for the empty paper cups. "Okay, sure."

"You will?" Her voice was pitched unnaturally high.

"Sure. What time should I pick you up?"

A dam arrived to pick up Cassie just as Jenna was on her way out to work, so they all walked to the parking lot together. Jenna was in a good mood, considering she had a long work shift ahead of her on the weekend.

"Tell me how the investigation goes," she said with a conspiratorial smile.

"This isn't for fun," Cassie said, glancing at Adam. "I'm just a concerned citizen."

"Hmm. I still want to hear everything later … Nancy."

Cassie glared at her roommate before turning away to find Adam holding the passenger door of his pickup for her.

"Nancy?" Adam arched an eyebrow.

She sighed. "Nancy Drew. She's teasing me."

"Ah."

Once she was seated, Adam closed the door and walked around to the driver's side. Cassie waited until they were out on the road to fill him in on the details she had learned so far.

"I want to get some more out of Lucy if I can. But I think several of those folks know more than they're saying. And if that's true, I think it's very possible that one or more of them could be in danger. Maybe someone needs a little encouragement to tell the police more. I just want them to be safe."

She rubbed her fingers together in her lap, wondering if he would think she was being too nosy.

But Adam just said, "I guess we start with Lucy, then. Just point out which place is hers."

Cassie looked up. They were on Maple Street. "Hey."

"What?"

"The white car is gone. Remember I told you about the Honda?"

"Yeah?"

"It was parked right there, but I noticed yesterday on my trash run that it was gone." She pointed.

"Hmm." Adam glanced at the now-empty spot. "I guess either the owner came and got it, or the police towed it."

They arrived at Silver Dawn a few minutes later, and Cassie directed him to Lucy's house.

Lucy emerged holding a coffee mug before they even had their doors closed.

"Cassie!" Lucy waved at her with her free hand. "This is a nice surprise. Who's the hunk?"

Cassie immediately felt her face color. "Lucy ..."

Adam chuckled and offered his hand to Lucy. "Call me Adam. Cassie and I work together."

"Ooh, how exciting," Lucy said. "Do you drive a truck too?"

"No," Adam said with an amused smile. "I'm on desk duty back at the office."

From Lucy's smirk, Cassie knew she wasn't referring to garbage collection as the exciting part. She wanted a subject change as soon as possible. "So, what are you doing this morning, Lucy?"

"Just this and that. As a matter of fact, I got a new window shade, and I'd like a hand putting it up if you can stop a minute. I'd hate to pass up having someone so tall and handsome to help out." She batted her eyelashes. "There's a cup of coffee in it for you."

"Sure, any friend of Cassie's," Adam said, smoothing over Cassie's mortification. "I won't say no to coffee, either."

Cassie told herself it was a good thing that Lucy seemed to like Adam right away. If she questioned her about her gambling now, either liking Adam would help her open up, or the serious subject would get her to stop teasing—a win either way.

Adam proved himself to be very handy with home maintenance, getting Lucy's new shade in place with relative ease.

When it was up and functioning, Lucy set mugs on her coffee table and smiled. "That's a job well done. I would have asked Hal's help, but between you and me,"—she dropped her voice to a loud whisper—"it probably would have taken him twice as long."

Cassie grinned and took up her mug. "Adam does seem good to have around," she said, choosing her words carefully. She noted that Lucy's notebooks were neatly stacked today, with no telltale racing notes in sight.

"Undoubtedly. Help yourself to creamer."

Adam came to sit on the sofa beside Cassie as Lucy took her seat in an armchair.

"And I think he's quite trustworthy," Cassie added.

"Hmm. That's good." Lucy's chipper voice took on a guarded edge.

"That's why I felt safe telling him about your little hobby."

"Oh, I see."

"No judgment," Adam put in. "Cassie just wanted more support for you. A fresh perspective."

He was better at this than Cassie had expected. She was pleased to see Lucy looking more relaxed already.

"Well, that's sweet," Lucy said.

Cassie picked up her mug. "I just wondered if there was

more to it than what you already told me. I want to know that you're not in any kind of trouble."

"I don't think so. I mean …" Lucy looked from Cassie to Adam and finally set her mug on a coaster. "The morning that you … found him … Jeff came by here early. I had just woken up myself, so I was already not in the best mood."

Cassie nodded in sympathy.

"He came to collect for his boss—that would be my … um … my bookie." She said it like it was a naughty word.

Adam frowned. "You use a bookie?"

Lucy's face flushed, and he gave Cassie a quick glance.

"Isn't that the usual way?" Cassie asked.

"No. Not nowadays. Most people do their betting online, I think. And even at racetracks, they use electronic devices and put down their deposit when they place the bet." Adam looked questioningly at their hostess.

"Yeah, see, I don't like that method," Lucy said. "If you work with a private bookie, you can just call and tell him what you want to put on a certain horse. Then, after the race, they get your winnings to you."

"What if you lose?" Cassie asked.

Lucy gave a little shrug. "I've been working with this man for a couple of years now, and he trusts me."

"So … you can run up a tab?" Adam asked.

"Not too much." Lucy squirmed a little and brushed back a curl. "I have a limit. If my losses total more than a thousand, I have to pay up before I can bet again."

Cassie puzzled over that. Last time they'd talked, Lucy had implied that she didn't owe much money. When she darted a glance at Adam, his eyebrows were pulled together and his mouth a grim line.

"Isn't that illegal?" he asked.

Lucy stiffened. "It's—I don't think so." She looked from Adam to Cassie, a sheen of fear showing in her eyes.

"I didn't think they were supposed to let you bet on—on speculation," Adam said.

"Uh, well, my guy's never had a problem with it. I think it varies from state to state."

Adam didn't seem happy. Cassie wondered if this was why Lucy wanted to keep Hal in the dark. She decided to move the conversation along.

"And you said Jeff came to see you early that morning?"

"Well, he never comes at a good time, and they like to collect in cash, so I gave him what I had in my pocketbook and told him he could get the rest next week. I was in my bathrobe, for heaven's sake! And the bank wasn't open yet."

"Was he okay with waiting for the rest?" asked Adam.

"No, he didn't like it. He said something like, 'You take care of yourself now. I hate to think what could happen in a sleepy little neighborhood like this,' or some such thing. I felt like I was in a gangster film."

Cassie's jaw dropped. "He really said that?"

Lucy nodded reluctantly. "He hadn't told me what time he was coming. I guess he expected me to have the cash all ready."

Adam scowled. "I'd think they'd want to keep a good relationship with their repeat customers."

"Yeah," Cassie said. "That wasn't too subtle. I'm pretty sure threatening someone like that *is* illegal."

Lucy gulped but said nothing.

"Did you see him leave?" Cassie asked.

Lucy nodded slowly. "Mm-hmm. But he didn't drive away. He walked on over to Ed and Flossie's."

"Did that seem weird? You don't think they have a similar arrangement with him, do you?"

"I really couldn't say." Lucy picked up her mug again and took a resigned slurp.

"Do you know when he left their house?" Adam prompted.

She shook her head. "I'm not sure …"

Cassie tried again. "You know we just want to help, Lucy. If you can remember anything else at all—"

"You should probably talk to Ed about it," Lucy interrupted.

Knowing Lucy, that was a clear *buzz-off* message, and Cassie knew they would learn nothing more from her today. "Well, thanks for talking to us."

"And thanks for the coffee," said Adam. He drained his mug. "It sounds like it's time for Cassie to introduce me to your neighbors."

"You were really good in there," Cassie said after Lucy saw them out of her home.

Pleased, Adam smiled. "I have to admit it is kind of fun being a concerned citizen. But I'm a little worried about your friend. I honestly think she's betting illegally. And if the guy threatened her ... Well, that's really rotten."

"Yeah."

He offered Cassie his arm. "Which one is Ed and Flossie's residence?"

Cassie took his arm and nodded toward one of the cookie-cutter homes.

"There. We can't say a word to them about Lucy's gambling, though."

"Right."

They crossed the distance in silence, and Adam rang the doorbell.

They heard movement inside, and soon Ed opened the door to them. "Good morning, Cassie," he said brightly. "And ..."

"Adam." He offered his hand. "I have the honor of escorting Cassie on her visiting this morning." He was getting into his role.

"Well, Flossie's off at Nita's shop at the moment, but you're welcome to come on in."

"If you don't mind," Cassie said.

They followed Ed to the sitting room and made themselves comfortable.

"Can I offer you anything?" their host asked.

"Thanks anyway," said Cassie. "We got coffee from Lucy already."

"I see. Making the rounds." He smiled.

"You might say that. To be honest, I'm kind of checking up on you folks. I've been a little worried, because a few of you seem to be connected to the … to Jeff."

"Oh." Ed shifted in his seat.

"Don't worry," Adam said, "I'm just here as Cassie's friend. I'm not going to blab anything you tell her to anyone else."

He nodded, still looking uncomfortable.

Cassie spoke slowly, as if she were choosing her words carefully. "The thing is, Lucy mentioned that she saw Jeff come over here that morning. The day it happened."

"Hmm. Well, I guess it's not a big secret. Like we told you, if everyone doesn't know we were related, they will soon." Ed paused a moment, then said, "The fact is, he came over here to ask us for money that day. He's asked us before."

"Have you given him money before?" Adam asked.

"Yes. Well, they were supposed to be loans, but he never made good on them. I'd about had it with that, so I told him we couldn't afford to lend him any more. He didn't like that. Started getting pretty offensive, actually. I didn't want to cave to that, but I didn't want him to start using foul language where Flossie could hear. I gave him twenty bucks and told him that was all I had on me."

"What did he do then?"

Ed hesitated. In the lull, they heard a car pull up, and Ed went to the window. "Flossie's back." He turned toward them. "Uh … after that, Jeff left. That's all."

Adam looked at Cassie. He could tell she thought the same as he did, that there was more to it than that, but it seemed that

Ed didn't want to proceed when Flossie was about to come through the door.

Flossie entered with a little blue bag sporting the words "Bead Dazzled" in swirly lettering. "Oh, it's you, Cassie," she said with a big smile. "Is that a new truck I saw at Lucy's?"

"It's mine, actually," Adam said, standing to greet her. "I'm Adam, Cassie's dispatcher and friend." The third introduction of the morning, this one felt like the best yet.

"Lovely to meet you." Flossie placed her thin little hand in his. "I was just down at Nita's shop getting some embroidery thread. And I may have picked up some charms while I was there." She added this with an apologetic look at her husband. "Everything is just so darling."

"Yes, yes," Ed said. "As long as you didn't fritter away the nest egg."

"Oh, you silly thing." Her eyes twinkled.

Cassie stood. "We should let you get on with your morning. Next time I come by, you can show me what you're working on, Flossie."

"I will," the older woman said. "Come anytime."

The couple walked Cassie and Adam to the door and said goodbye.

"They're sweet." Adam offered his arm to Cassie again.

"They really are," Cassie agreed.

Adam said no more, but he hoped he could be happily married at Ed's age. And possibly that his wife might be Cassie. She was sweet too. He liked so many things about her—she was easy to talk to, and she let him open doors for her. Church was important to her, and she showed concern for her elderly friends. He found her love of mystery novels endearing.

"So," he said when they were on the road again in his truck, "do you feel better or worse based on what we learned?"

"Worse, to be honest," Cassie said. "I have more of the picture now, but I think I'm missing a lot. And I still think Lucy and Ed both know more than they said."

"I thought so too. That Lucy probably knew full well she was acting outside the law. Gambling is highly regulated now."

"Yeah. I'm not up on all that, and I don't see why she doesn't just place her bets on her laptop or her phone."

"Maybe she's not very tech-savvy. But I think it's like she said. She doesn't want to have to pay up front."

"But if she gets behind, that bookie sends Jeff to collect her debt. Does that mean she's at least a thousand dollars behind right now?"

Adam sighed. "I think so. At least she was before she gave him a partial payment that morning."

"But when we talked to her the other day, she said she wasn't really in debt. A thousand is a lot. Especially for seniors on a fixed income."

"She probably didn't want you to know."

Cassie's phone pinged, and she took it from her pocket. "Jenna texted. She wants an update."

Adam waited while Cassie answered her text message.

After a minute, she said, "She wants to *discuss the clues* tonight." She made quote marks in the air with her fingers. "You want to have supper with us later? We'll just make pasta or something."

The idea of spending more of his day off with Cassie required little consideration. "Sure, why not?"

CHAPTER NINE

"Okay, so what do we actually know about this Jeff guy?" Adam asked as the three sat around the kitchen table in the apartment.

Cassie speared a meatball with her fork. "He was Ed Simonson's cousin's boy."

"Right. Do you think Ed would kill his own relative?"

"No. I don't think any of the folks at Silver Dawn would kill anyone." Cassie popped the meatball into her mouth. She and Jenna had collaborated on preparing the meal. Adam had arrived a few minutes early, and he'd pitched in by slicing the cucumber for the salad. Everything had seemed friendly and lighthearted, but now they were getting down to the serious stuff.

He leaned forward. "Jeff was some sort of henchman for a bookie. We know that from what Lucy told us. And he frequently asked Ed for loans that he never repaid."

Jenna frowned. "We're talking about the dead guy from the dumpster, right?"

Cassie nodded. "Some of the folks at Silver Dawn seemed as if they were holding back on us. I think Lucy in particular was scared of him. But I don't think she killed him. No way."

"Somebody was mad enough at him to kill him." Adam reached for the ranch dressing.

"Maybe he was skimming from the bookie," Jenna said. "Travis told me that guy worked for a crime boss."

"Really?" Cassie was surprised Travis would tell his girlfriend details about an ongoing criminal investigation. "Is he working on this case now?"

"Not exactly, but he heard about it."

"Okay," Adam said. "Is a bookie the same as a crime boss, or are we talking about two different people here?"

Jenna shrugged. "I didn't hear anything about the bookie."

"Well, I did a little reading this afternoon, and supposedly most bookies nowadays aren't Mafia dons or anything like that. Most operate independently."

"But it could be." Jenna's voice held a stubborn note.

"I suppose."

"Maybe the crime boss is higher up than the bookie. He could have had several people working under him." Cassie looked over at Adam as he poured dressing over his salad. "We need to know what sort of stuff Jeff did for this crime boss. I mean, obviously he collected gambling debts. Anything else?"

"That may have been enough to keep him busy," Adam said. "Since we're so close to the racetrack, I mean."

Jenna lowered her voice. "I was told he also collected on drug deals."

"What?" Cassie stared at her.

Jenna nodded, her eyes huge.

"This Jeff guy was a drug dealer?"

With a shrug, Jenna picked up her garlic bread. "I got the impression it was more that he would carry the money from the dealers to the boss. He was Ollie Schwam's runner."

Adam's forked clattered on his plate. "Ollie Schwam? Are you sure?"

"You've heard of him?" Jenna asked.

Cassie just stared at them. "Well, I haven't. Who is he?"

"He's notorious," Adam said. "I had no idea he had dealings here in this little town. I thought he stuck to the big city."

"Must be expanding. Please don't tell anyone else. I don't think I was supposed to talk about him." Jenna took a big bite of her bread.

"Cassie, listen to me." Adam looked into her eyes, and she could tell he was dead serious. "That guy is dangerous. You need to keep away from him. We shouldn't even have gone asking questions about Jeff."

"How would Ollie Schwam know what we're doing?"

"Oh, he'll find out, especially if you keep sniffing around. You've got to let the police handle it."

Cassie didn't like being told what to do, but Adam sounded genuinely concerned, so she didn't argue.

"Oh, I guess I can tell you," Jenna said. "Trav said they towed that car you took the pictures of."

"I wondered," Cassie said.

Jenna reached for the salad dressing. "Yeah. It was the victim's."

Cassie stared at her. "So, he drove it to Silver Dawn on Friday, and ... and possibly someone moved it outside the complex later?"

"Possibly," Adam said, his forehead wrinkled. "Maybe somebody didn't want it to be found inside Silver Dawn."

When he left an hour later, Cassie was still thinking about Jeff Patterson. He'd been involved in some really bad stuff. Was she wrong about the seniors? Had one of them shot Jeff to protect Lucy from him and his boss, Ollie Schwam? Maybe Hal had found out about her gambling and was afraid for her. If he thought Lucy was in danger, would he shoot the man who was threatening her? Hal really liked Lucy. He'd probably do anything to keep her safe.

Or maybe Ed got tired of Jeff hitting him up for money. Cassie didn't think he'd strike back so violently, but what if she was wrong? How well did she know Ed—or any of the others, for that matter?

And what about Jeff's car? Had Gerald or somebody else moved it so attention wouldn't be drawn to the seniors at Silver Dawn? And the young fellows looking in the dumpster—were they significant?

She lay awake for a long time that night with her head spinning.

On Sunday morning, Cassie awoke bleary-eyed, her mind still troubled. Jenna eyed her closely when she entered the kitchen.

"You okay?"

"Yeah, I just didn't sleep very well."

"Thinking about the murder?"

Cassie grimaced. "I couldn't shut it down last night."

Jenna reached for the coffeepot. "Here. Fresh brew may help. You're not playing the piano today, are you?"

"No. Mrs. Paulette's got it covered this morning."

"Good." Jenna poured a mug nearly full of black coffee and set it before Cassie. For her own serving, she left an inch for plenty of milk. "I'm boiling a couple of eggs. Want one?"

"Sure. Sounds good." Cassie took a sip of coffee. Too hot. She set down the mug and rose to start the toast. "Where's the bread?" Her gaze lit on the empty spot near the toaster.

"We're out," Jenna said with a wince. "Sorry. I thought we'd stop at the store on the way home from church and grab a loaf."

"Okay." Cassie opened the refrigerator's freezer compartment. "What else we got?"

"You might find some bagels in there if you root around."

Cassie shuffled some of the packages of frozen berries, veggies, and burgers, and came up with a six-pack of blueberry bagels. "Perfect."

As they put their dirty dishes in the dishwasher later, she

smiled at Jenna. "You were right. I haven't thought about Jeff Patterson for fifteen minutes."

"That's progress. See if you can focus on the Sunday school lesson."

That was easier said than done. Adam met them in the hallway outside their classroom and sat next to Cassie in the second row of folding chairs. Her thoughts weren't always on the murder, though. It was funny how her pulse ratcheted up a notch every time Adam smiled at her. *Stop that!* She gazed down at her open Bible. *Mephibosheth. Think about him.*

She did better during the worship service. Travis and Adam sat like bookends to her and Jenna. When the service was over, Jenna was set to go off with Travis to have lunch with his parents.

"You want to get something to eat?" Adam asked Cassie.

"Sure. That'd be great. But we have to get a loaf of bread afterward."

They chose Cassie's favorite Chinese restaurant and soon were eating shrimp pot stickers, orange chicken, and kung pao beef. They shared their meals, but Cassie found the beef dish too spicy and stuck to her chicken and fried rice.

"This is really good. Thanks for bringing me here." With her chopsticks, she chose another nugget of savory chicken.

"You're welcome." Adam's smile made her pulse flutter. Even so, she couldn't keep her mind from straying back to the thing that occupied her most.

A few minutes later, Adam jerked her back to the here and now. "You're thinking about the murder, aren't you?"

Her cheeks heated, and she quickly swallowed her bite of rice. "How could you tell?"

"I think it was the unfocused yet deadly serious look on your face. I don't know of anything else that would preoccupy you like that."

"Guilty as charged." She laid her chopsticks on her plate. "I'd really like to talk to Ed again."

"No."

"What do you mean, no?" She arched her eyebrows at him.

"You can't go out there again."

She scrunched up her face in an exaggerated frown. She didn't like Adam taking such a bossy tone when they weren't at work. "I hate to wait until my next trash run."

He leaned toward her. "If you start talking to them when you're on your route, you'll mess up the entire day's schedule. I know what happens when you start talking to those people. It goes on and on."

Cassie gazed at him for a moment in silence. "You sound like Mac, over the radio."

Adam's shoulders slumped. "I don't want to be that guy right now. We're not at work. It's Sunday."

"Which is exactly why I can go over to Silver Dawn and chat with my friends without it interfering with work."

Adam sighed. "Can't we just enjoy this time together?"

After a moment's consideration, she arched her eyebrows. "I think I'd enjoy more time with you anywhere, but especially at Silver Dawn."

"What about your loaf of bread?" he asked feebly.

Cassie grinned. "That's easy. There's a convenience store right around the corner from the entrance to the Silver Dawn community. Come on. What do you say?"

Adam looked around as though he desperately sought a diversion. "How about ice cream?"

"I'm really full, but thanks. You get some if you want it."

"That's okay. But, hey, we haven't opened our fortune cookies yet." His big, blue eyes almost melted her.

"Right," she said.

At the same time, they both reached for the small tray that held two fortune cookies, and their hands brushed. Cassie flinched a little and then gave herself a mental kick. She grasped the nearest cookie's wrapper and opened it.

Adam unwrapped the other one and nodded. "You go first.

She broke the crisp shell, scattering crumbs over her plate as she pulled out the strip of paper. "Hmm, that's interesting."

"What's it say?"

She met Adam's gaze. "Follow your heart today."

His brow wrinkled. "Really?"

"Well, I might have added the *today*." She nodded toward the cookie in his hand. "What does yours say?"

He kept a poker face as he opened it. "Listen to those you love." His face went scarlet.

Cassie stared at him. Why was he embarrassed? Did Adam love her? Maybe he didn't want to admit it. But it was too soon, really. They hadn't known each other long enough. Maybe he was afraid she would think it meant he loved her and should listen to her but didn't want that.

She cleared her throat. "These sound more like an advice column than fortunes."

Adam looked away. "They do that sometimes."

"Well, I think it should say, *All will go well today*, or *You'll meet someone interesting soon*, something like that."

He stuffed the two cookie pieces into his mouth and crunched them. Was he trying to avoid discussing the fortunes?

She waited patiently until he'd swallowed the remnants of the cookie with a slosh of root beer.

"So? What now?"

"Aren't you going to eat yours?" he asked.

"No, thanks."

"Will your fortune still come true if you don't?"

She laughed. "I've never heard that one before."

"Oh, come on. It's like blowing out the birthday candles. If you don't get them all in one breath, your wish won't come true."

She studied him keenly. "You're stalling."

Adam reached for his glass but stopped with his hand in midair. "You're right." He met her gaze. "I can't talk you out of going, can I?"

"I don't think so. If you don't want to be there, I can go on my own."

"No, don't do that."

She had to fight a smile when she saw resignation on his face.

Twenty minutes later, they rolled through the entrance gate at Silver Dawn. Adam had given up his protests, but he still wore an expression that said, *Why do I let myself get talked into these things?* As they approached Ed and Flossie's neat little house, she noted that the red-and-white petunias were taking hold. They really cheered up the place, and she wouldn't have guessed they'd been planted less than a week before.

An image crossed her mind of all the friends gathered in the yard to help with the planting. Hal had swept the walkway. Was he just brushing away loose soil that had spilled over onto the concrete? But then Gerald had gone over the surface with a ... a mop. She hadn't thought much about it at the time because they'd jumped into a conversation about the dumpster. But what was in Gerald's bucket? Plain water? Or was it some kind of cleaning product? She couldn't remember smelling anything odd at the time.

But why would anyone feel the need to wash a walkway? That did seem odd. Had there been a jug sitting on the bottom step leading up to the porch? A white jug—or was she imagining it? She'd heard Travis talk about witnesses with false memories. And yet ...

She shivered despite the warm sun on her shoulders.

Adam put on the parking brake and unclasped his seatbelt. As he reached for his door handle, Cassie grabbed his right wrist.

"Wait."

"What is it?" He turned to face her.

"I just remembered something. I came here the other day. Monday, when I was off duty."

"Okaaay."

She pressed her lips tightly together, then plunged into the scene she'd found at the Simonsons' house that day—neighbors helping to plant the flowerbeds, Hal sweeping the walk, and Gerald with the bucket and mop. And the possibility of a bleach bottle on the steps.

"Adam, I think ..." She swallowed hard. "I think Jeff Patterson died right there in front of Ed and Flossie's house."

CHAPTER
TEN

E ven if Cassie's hunch was wrong, Adam was sure that nothing short of a straight answer would satisfy her. Much as he didn't want her getting involved, it seemed that she already was. All he could do was support her. His stepfather, Sean, had told him when dating Adam's mother, "If you can't change her mind, at least try to make sure she doesn't get hurt following her heart." The philosophy seemed to apply here.

"Ready?" he asked as they walked up to Ed and Flossie's door together.

"I guess."

Adam rang the doorbell, and they waited. Unlike their previous visit, no one opened the door, and there was no sound from inside. "Should I ring again?"

Cassie nodded.

After another ring and another minute of waiting, Cassie turned to look around. "I guess neither of them is home this time."

"So, what now?"

"Gerald's over in his yard. We could try talking to him."

Adam followed Cassie's gaze and saw the elderly man

adjusting solar lights along his driveway. "Might as well give it a try."

Cassie introduced Adam to Gerald and asked the retiree what he was up to.

"These stake lights keep tipping this way and that. I thought maybe the ground was just shifting with the weather, but I'm starting to think my cat likes to bat them over."

"Cats do get into mischief," Adam said.

"Speaking of mischief, I keep wondering about that man who was killed," said Cassie.

Subtle. Adam looked at Gerald's face.

The older man appeared uneasy already. "Yeah, I guess we all do."

Cassie went on. "Specifically, I wondered why he was in the dumpster in the first place. It's pretty obvious someone put him there."

"You think so?" Gerald moved to the next light and leaned down to straighten it.

"The thing is … after he was found, the next time I came by, a bunch of you were working on Ed and Flossie's walk. Planting things, cleaning up … remember?"

Gerald didn't look at her. "I remember."

"I believe someone had brought out bleach for the walkway. You were mopping, right?"

"Maybe. Someone was. I guess I might o' done some mopping."

"Were you trying to get rid of a blood stain?"

Gerald finally looked her in the eye. "What are you talking about?"

"We're not here to accuse you of anything," Adam put in.

"Right," said Cassie. "I'd understand you wanting to help out your friends and not ask too many questions."

"I don't know what you mean. Nothing was going on." Gerald's pitch rose in agitation.

"Gerald, I just want to help. But it's downright silly to use bleach on a walkway if there isn't a really persistent stain there. So, please don't insult my intelligence."

Adam was surprised at the scolding tone Cassie took on.

Apparently, it worked. Gerald looked away with a little groan and then admitted, "Fine. You're right. That Friday morning, before you came around, I heard what I thought was a gunshot, but maybe it was a backfire. It took me a minute to get out there to see what happened, and there was Ed in his undershirt, standing over a dead man. Right on his front walk. But he didn't have his gun. I'd swear to that."

Adam held back the questions he wanted to ask, letting Gerald go at his own pace.

"Well, Flossie came running out a minute later. I guess she heard it too. Ed said someone shot Jeff and we should all get inside and call the police. But Flossie said they would think Ed did it because they'd complained about Jeff before. She was sure he'd get arrested, and it would take a long time and maybe a lawyer they couldn't afford to prove him innocent."

Gerald paused, seeming not to want to go on.

"What did you think happened?" Cassie asked.

"To be honest … I guess I really thought Ed did it when I first saw him. But like I said, he didn't have his gun. And he was adamant that someone else ran off between those two houses across the way." He pointed across the cul-de-sac. "He didn't see him very clearly, but he said it was a man wearing black. I think he was telling the truth."

Adam was skeptical. *Wearing black? That's it?*

"Then Hal and Lucy showed up. Lucy freaked out—just about fainted when she saw the body. Hal asked if we'd called the police, and then Flossie started crying, all 'They'll arrest my husband if we do that.' So, we talked it over a while, kind of panicky to be honest, and then someone said we should just get Jeff off Ed and Flossie's doorstep. Ed had a wheelbarrow, and the dumpster was nearby, so …" Gerald bit his lip.

"And you *knew* he was in there when I came to make my pickup," Cassie said, sounding upset for the first time.

"I'm sorry about that. I guess I was kind of hoping you wouldn't notice ..."

"Wouldn't notice?"

Adam put his hand on Cassie's shoulder. "They were probably in shock. People don't think clearly when things like this happen."

"That's true," said Gerald. "We didn't think about how it would affect Cassie. Or—or what would happen to the body."

"How about the cleanup?" asked Cassie. "You must have done some of it on Friday."

"Yes, Ed did that while we scrubbed out the wheelbarrow. But Sunday, Flossie noticed some blood Ed missed on the walk, plus a bit of a stain from the part he already cleaned. Ed bought some flowers so we'd have a cover for the cleaning. I brought the bleach over, and we went at it again."

Cassie eyed him sternly. "You really need to tell this to the police."

Gerald looked more uncomfortable than ever. "But they'll think we all had something to hide. We could get charged with being accessories or ... something. I don't know."

"I think they'll be lenient if you volunteer the information," said Adam. "And you're all telling the truth, so having so many witnesses is a good thing."

"I don't think the others will go for it. Ed and Flossie sure won't."

"How about if we talk to everyone and find out?" asked Cassie. "We'll start with Lucy. If everyone agrees, will you come clean?"

After a moment of consideration, Hal nodded. "All right. But only if it's unanimous."

"Good. Operation Unanimous, here we come."

Cassie waited until she and Adam were out of Gerald's hearing to say, "Don't these people watch cop shows? Don't they know how bad it looks if you cover something up, especially if it has to do with a murder?"

"I think we've all done things that seemed like a good idea at the time, even though we knew better," Adam said.

"I guess." She wondered if he felt guilty about being harsh with her over the radio, or if he had other regrets.

She led the way over to Lucy's house.

When Lucy opened the door, she looked pleased to see them. Cassie almost didn't want to bring up Jeff now, but she knew that another opportunity might not come for a while.

"Cassie! And … Adam, right? Come in. Coffee?"

Adam shrugged. "Sure, if it's no trouble."

Lucy ushered them into her sitting room again and went to her modest kitchen to start up the coffeemaker. "It's nice you came again so soon," she called.

Cassie raised her voice. "I wish it were a purely social visit."

"Uh-oh." Lucy stepped through the wide doorway. "That sounds ominous. What's going on?"

"I guess I'll cut right to the chase. I know why you were all working on Ed and Flossie's walk last week."

Lucy's face froze for a moment. Then she uttered a soft, "Oh."

"I get why no one wanted the police to know that's where Jeff was killed, but I think it was a mistake not to tell them."

"Sugar, who told you?" Lucy moved back to lean against the doorframe. "No one was supposed to know. We said, 'If everyone keeps their mouths shut, nothing will come of it.' And now someone blabbed. I just knew this would happen."

Cassie scrunched up her face. "I kind of figured it out myself and pressured someone to confirm it, actually."

"I should probably have made tea, not coffee. My stomach's in knots. Oh, dear."

Adam and Cassie tried to reassure Lucy, telling her about the plan for everyone to bring their evidence forward together.

"But we moved the—well, I didn't really move it, but the fellows did, and I stood there and watched. Isn't it tampering with evidence? Won't we all get in a heap of trouble?"

"There may be some trouble," Adam said, "but not as much as if the police figure this out on their own. In the long run, being truthful will be much better for everyone."

"If I could figure it out, you can bet they will," Cassie added.

"Oh, I don't know, I don't know." Lucy skittered back into the kitchen and returned a minute later with three mugs on a tray with some creamer.

"How did you get involved with Mr. Schwam in the first place?" Cassie asked as Lucy set down the tray.

"Mr. Who? I thought his name was Patterson."

"It is. Was." Cassie threw a glance at Adam, hoping he could help her out.

"Jeff worked for a bookie," Adam said. "Didn't you know his name?"

"No. I kind of thought if I didn't know too much about him, he wouldn't know about me, either. It was all done over the phone. When I wanted to bet, I'd call him. And then Jeff would come get my money or bring me whatever I'd won. Or I'd call and have them use my winnings for another bet."

"But ... how did you know where to call?" Cassie asked, trying to puzzle it out.

"Jeff. He saw me using a lottery ticket one day. You know, one of those scratch cards. He'd been to see Ed, I think, and he noticed me on my porch. He just sauntered over and started talking about winning it big. After a bit of conversation, he asked if I ever went to the racetrack. I admitted I do now and then. Well, he told me I could do my betting anonymously."

"He's the one who put you in touch with the bookie," Adam said.

"Yes." Lucy looked at Cassie. "What did you say his name was?"

Cassie opened her mouth, but Adam cut in.

"It may be better if you don't know. When the time comes, just tell the police everything you've told us."

Lucy took a big gulp of her coffee.

Before Cassie could say anything else, Lucy turned the conversation back to the murder. "I admit, when I first saw that Jeff was dead that day ... well, I was shocked, of course, but also kind of glad. Isn't that terrible? But I thought, at least he wouldn't bother me anymore."

"I think that's understandable," Adam said.

"But then I started wondering if Hal found out he'd been harassing me and decided to do something about it. I believed what Ed told us about the stranger, but I just wasn't sure about my sweetie. Supposing he got dressed up in black for a disguise and killed Jeff to protect me? He's such a gentleman."

This had not occurred to Cassie. "You don't think he'd really do that, do you?"

"No ... no, not really. But in case he did, I was willing to help the others hide the evidence. That sounds really bad, doesn't it?"

"It doesn't sound good." Cassie tried to picture Hal in black sweats and a ski mask. She just couldn't see him doing such a thing. "Maybe we should just ask Hal about it directly."

"But that would mean telling him my secret!" Lucy looked into her mug, stirring in creamer like her life depended on it. "No. No, no."

Cassie softened her tone. "Hal should probably know about it anyway, Lucy. It's not good to keep things from someone you care about. And if Hal really cares about you, it won't make him stop. He's a good guy, right?"

"Well, yes. Of course."

"And you wouldn't think so anymore if he were willing to shoot a man rather than confronting him, right?"

"I guess not," Lucy said. "It is a bit stupid to protect a murderer, isn't it?"

"So, you can explain things and give him the chance to proclaim his innocence."

"I don't know, Cassie. You're asking an awful lot."

They fell silent for a few minutes. Cassie tried to appreciate Lucy's position, but she knew what she believed to be right in this case.

Adam finally spoke.

"I think maybe we should just call everyone together whenever Ed and Flossie get back. We wanted to convince them each individually, but now I'm thinking that just makes you feel isolated."

Lucy took a sip of her coffee and looked up at him. "Yes, I think you're right. I don't like being in the hot seat."

"Okay. Cassie, what do you say we go back to Gerald's and let him know we're having a powwow?" Adam eyed her expectantly.

Since this idea was still in line with their plan and seemed to appeal to the reluctant Lucy, Cassie relented. "All right. I'm sure Ed and Flossie won't be gone all day. Let's go tell him."

"Thank you, dear," said Lucy. "I'll keep an ear out for Ed's car." She walked them to the door and hugged Cassie before they left. "It's really sweet of you to want to help."

Cassie hoped Lucy's perception of her was accurate and she wasn't motivated more by her curiosity than by a neighborly spirit.

CHAPTER
ELEVEN

"I hate to leave her alone," Cassie said as she and Adam ambled down Lucy's front walk. She's so upset."

"These people have got to realize they can't hold back evidence from the police." Adam frowned. "They could all end up in jail for obstructing an investigation."

"Do you really think so?" Cassie felt as though a giant was squeezing her lungs. "They're too old to go to jail."

"Age makes no difference," Adam said.

She clamped her lips together. As soon as she'd realized her friends were hiding a huge secret, she'd feared they'd all be in legal hot water. She could ask Travis what he thought would happen—but no. Travis was an officer, and if she told him any of this, he'd have to report it. She stopped walking and gazed up at Adam. "What are we going to do?"

He huffed out a breath and reached for her hand. "I know it's not what you want to hear, but now that we know at least part of what happened, if we don't come clean on this we could be in trouble too."

Cassie swallowed hard and gazed around at the cluster of neat little bungalows. A white car was turning into a driveway on the other side of the cul-de-sac. "That's Nita's car. She must be just getting home."

"Is her bead shop open on Sunday?"

"I don't think so. Maybe she's been out with friends." She met Adam's sober gaze. "They're all home now, other than Ed and Flossie. Can we call them all together and lay it out to them? The danger they're in, I mean. The seriousness of what they've done."

"We need to."

"Do you think we can keep Lucy's secret, about the gambling?"

"I doubt it. It has to come out eventually."

"But for now?"

Adam sighed. "For now, I guess we can keep that quiet. Let her tell it when she's ready."

Cassie pointed toward the next house. "Gerald's still in his yard."

"Good." Adam strode confidently toward the older man.

Gerald waved and gave them a halfhearted smile. "What did Lucy have to say?"

They walked up close to him so they wouldn't have to yell, and Cassie told him, "Lucy didn't want to admit that any of you knew anything about it, but when we told her we knew some of your friends group was involved, she admitted it—reluctantly."

"I see."

"She told us some of you moved the body," Adam said. "She realizes that was wrong, and that somebody should have reported Jeff's death to the police, but she's scared."

"I don't blame her." Gerald shook his head. "I'm a little scared myself."

Cassie eyed him intently. "You said Lucy almost fainted. Why do you think that was?"

"I guess I thought it was because of all the blood. And ... and she probably knew Jeff. I mean, he's been around the neighborhood before.

"Did she know he was related to Ed?"

"I have no idea," Gerald said. "I knew, but I'm not sure if everyone else did."

"Okay, well, we want to get everyone together and talk about this. Can we do that at your house?"

"Sure. I mean, it's kind of small, but I think I have enough chairs. How many people are we talking about?"

"Well, you and Ed, Flossie, Hal, and Lucy, for sure," Adam replied. "Anyone else you think should be there?"

Gerald sighed. "Nita was in on it too. She knew about the body, and she helped us cover up what we were doing. Stood watch while we got him into the wheelbarrow and put him in the dumpster."

"Okay," Cassie said. "We'll go and invite her. We'll start the meeting as soon as Ed and Flossie get home."

"Right. I'll go put on some coffee and put the kitchen chairs in the living room."

Gerald headed into his house while Cassie and Adam walked across the circle to Nita's house.

"Hey, Cassie!"

She cringed at the sound of her name. Not the person she wanted to run into just now. She and Adam paused on the sidewalk and turned toward Kieran.

"Hi, Kieran." He marched up to them and gazed at Adam with what Cassie felt was a hostile gaze.

Does he think I'm bringing more trouble to Silver Dawn? Surely he's not jealous! Uneasily, she recalled his invitation to a karaoke party.

"This is Adam MacAllister," she said. "Adam, this is Kieran Harmon. He's the maintenance man here at Silver Dawn, and his dad is superintendent of the complex."

"Hello," Adam said.

Kieran gave a curt nod and focused on Cassie. "I was hoping to see you again. I've been taking guitar lessons, and I bought a new folk guitar. You wanna see it?"

"Uh, not right now, Kieran."

He scowled. "Yeah, well maybe next time you come for the garbage."

Before Cassie could respond, Adam said, "When Cassie's driving the truck, she's supposed to stay on her work schedule, not stop to chat."

Even though he sounded a bit like Mac, Cassie knew he was right, and she didn't mind him being a bit stern with Kieran.

Kieran's eyebrows lowered. "Well, she's not on her work schedule now, is she? I don't see any truck."

She dredged up something she hoped resembled a smile. "No, I'm not, but we do have some personal business that we need to take care of. Sorry."

Turning away, she wondered how smart it was to go straight to Nita's house. If Kieran was feeling vengeful, he might keep watching and try to figure out what rated as her "personal business."

"Come on," Adam muttered, taking her hand. "That guy has a chip on his shoulder."

"He does. Thanks for stepping up. And I'll try to remember about the schedule."

Adam grimaced. "I wasn't trying to come down on you."

"I know." Cassie rang the bell, and before she expected it, Nita flung open the door.

"Hi, Cassie. What's up? I saw you two making the rounds."

"Hey, Nita." Cassie tried to smile, but she wasn't feeling very cheerful just now. "This is Adam MacAllister. He's a friend of mine, and he's a dispatcher at Reuben's Rubbish Removal, where I work."

Nita eyed him soberly. "Hello."

"Pleased to meet you," Adam said.

Cassie cleared her throat. "We'd like to have a meeting over at Gerald's house—him and you and the Simonsons, as well as Hal and Lucy."

"What for?"

"To talk about Jeff Patterson."

"Who? Oh, you mean the dead guy."

"Did you know him?" Cassie asked.

"Sort of. He stole money from my shop once. Held me at gunpoint."

Cassie's jaw dropped.

"I'm glad you're okay," Adam said. "You called the police, of course?"

"Oh, yeah. And they got him." Nita's lips skewed in distaste. "I had to go in and pick him out of a lineup. He never came back to the shop again, but every now and then, I'd see him walking across the complex, and I'd wonder if he was here to rob people. Every time I saw him, I hid. Couldn't help it—that guy scared me."

Cassie nodded. "I don't blame you,"

Adam said, "Did you know he was related to Ed Simonson?"

"What? No." Nita huffed out a breath. "So why do you want to hold a meeting about him?"

Cassie glanced at Adam, and he gave her a tiny nod. "It seems you and several of your neighbors knew Jeff's body was in the dumpster when I came last Friday."

"They told you, huh?" Nita's face looked a little gray.

"Yes," Cassie said. "Are you all right?"

Nita waved a hand through the air in dismissal. "Yeah, I'm fine. But that's when I found out about him. It was quite a shock. When I went out early that morning, I saw some of my friends over near Ed and Flossie's house. I strolled over to see what happened, and he was lying there on the walkway." She swallowed hard.

"What did they tell you?"

Nita met her gaze, her face stricken. "It was awful. I hate to admit it, but I thought at first Ed had shot him. If he tried to break in or something, you know?"

"What do you think now?" Adam asked.

"I—I don't know what to think. I mean, Ed's a good guy,

and ... but ..." Nita stared helplessly at Cassie. "If they're related, who knows what happened? And I—I helped them dispose of the body."

She swayed, and Cassie and Adam both reached out to steady her.

"Easy, now," Adam said.

"Let's go over to Gerald's and sit down and talk about this," Cassie said. "He's making coffee."

"I could use a cup." Nita came out onto the porch and locked her front door behind her.

A white Trailblazer rolled down the street and curved around the cul-de-sac.

"Isn't that Ed and Flossie?" Cassie said.

Nita looked at the moving SUV. "Yeah, that's them."

"You gals go ahead over to Gerald's," Adam said. "I'll go invite the Simonsons."

Ten minutes later, the group of friends were gathered in Gerald's living room. Everyone who had been on hand when the body fell from the dumpster into Cassie's truck, with the exception of Kieran, was present. Lucy helped the host serve coffee.

When they all had their mugs, Cassie cleared her throat.

"Okay, everyone, we've established that you all knew about Jeff Patterson's death last Friday, and in fact helped move his body and later cover up the evidence."

Hal pulled a face. "You make us sound like criminals."

"No," Cassie said. "I know you're not. But Jeff Patterson was a criminal. And, Ed, I know he was your cousin, and I'm sorry, but I think we all agree Jeff was into some pretty bad stuff."

The older people nodded, not quite meeting her gaze.

"You have to tell the police what happened," Cassie said.

Everyone started protesting, shaking their heads and talking over each other. Cassie couldn't make out any rational sentences.

Adam put his thumb and forefinger to his mouth and gave a sharp whistle. At once, the cacophony stilled.

"Folks, we understand how upsetting this is, and that you're frightened. Nobody wants to get in trouble. But really, you need to do this."

Ed's Adam's apple bobbed as he swallowed. "I know you're right." He glanced questioningly at Flossie.

"If you think we should, honey," she said shakily and reached for Ed's hand.

"You should," Cassie said. "If you want, we can ask for an officer to come here, and we'll stay with you if they'll let us." She gazed around at the group and looked pointedly at each face. "You need to tell them the *whole* truth."

"What if one of us ends up in jail?" Nita demanded.

"Or more than one?" Gerald added.

Lucy grimaced. "Yeah. They could throw us all in the hoosegow."

"I don't think they'll do that," Cassie said.

Ed eyed her shrewdly. "But you don't know for sure."

"Well, no. I can't say for certain. But Adam and I will stand by you and make sure you're treated fairly."

"Fairly?" Flossie's voice rose in panic. "Is what we did a crime? If it is, I don't want to be treated fairly."

Hal scowled at Ed. "We shouldn't have done it, and we all know it."

Ed held up both hands helplessly. "I didn't force you to help."

In exasperation, Cassie turned toward Adam. As she did so, a shadow at the window moved.

"Adam," she hissed. "There's someone outside."

He whipped around to look, rose, and walked to the window.

"What is it?" Gerald asked.

"A man was out there," Adam said. "I think he was looking in the window at us. I saw him slink away toward the gate."

Gerald jumped up and hurried to stand beside him. "I don't see anyone."

"He's gone now," Adam told him.

Cassie stood. "Look, friends, let's leave this overnight."

"Really?" Adam said. "Do you think that's wise?"

"No. I think we should tell the police today. But if some of you need more time ..." She looked over the group, and her heart ached for these dear people. "I'll come back tomorrow afternoon. But you all think about it. Because telling the police is the right thing to do."

Hal muttered something under his breath, and Nita sneaked a look at Ed, but nobody refuted what Cassie said.

Climbing back into Adam's pickup was a big relief, and Cassie inhaled deeply as she tightened her seat belt.

"You okay?" Adam asked as he started the engine.

"Yeah."

"We should do something fun now."

She smiled at that. "Do you know if the racetrack is open today?"

"What? The racetrack? You're kidding, right?"

"Only halfway. I'd really like to go there."

"Whatever for?"

"I like horses, and ..."

Adam frowned. "And what?"

"Okay, I'd like to try to learn more about Jeff's connection to the bookie."

"That's crazy. You can't just go out there and start questioning unsavory people. It's not safe."

"There'd be lots of people around."

"Yeah, but I don't think this bookie works at the track, remember? He does his business under the table." Adam braked for a stop sign. "Anyway, I don't want you to take risks."

"I'd have you there." She raised her eyebrows and smiled. "I'd really like to see the track and find out how things work there, and I do love horses."

"I doubt if they're open today, and the afternoon is waning."

Adam waited for a couple of cars to pass. "There's someplace else we could go for a little while, if you'd like."

"Where?"

"Well, do you like dogs too?"

"Yes, but I haven't had one since I was little. It was my dad's dog, actually. A beagle. We called him Barkley." Fond memories of the beloved pet relaxed Cassie a bit.

His face relaxed. "I volunteer at the animal shelter in town."

"Really?" That perked up her interest.

"Yeah, just once or twice a week, when I have time. I like to play with the dogs and cuddle the puppies."

"Aw." Something else about Adam she hadn't known. She liked this side of him.

His smile grew bigger. "You want to go meet some of my furry friends?"

"I'd love to."

"Great. We can grab a pizza or something after for our supper."

"I'm in!"

"And maybe we can talk about how we'll make sure your senior buddies will follow through and talk to the police about the body."

"Uh-uh," she cautioned. "Let's not talk about it now. We're going to have fun, remember?"

"Right." But Adam's face remained sober as he headed the truck toward the animal shelter.

CHAPTER
TWELVE

C assie was much more distracted from current events when her phone rang and she saw who was calling.

"Oh, it's my mother. I don't know why she'd be calling ..."

"You can take it if you want," Adam said.

"Okay. Sorry." She flicked her finger over her screen and put the phone to her ear. "Hello."

"Cassandra."

Cassie winced. This use of her name in this tone told her the way this conversation was going to go, and now wasn't a great time. She tried to keep her own tone light. "Hi, Mom. What's up?"

"I haven't heard from you in weeks. Now I find out someone in your area found a *body* in a dumpster! Tell me you quit that awful job."

She hoped Adam couldn't hear her mother. "Actually, no. But it's fine. The police are handling it. It really doesn't affect my job."

"How can you say that? It's a clear sign that you're not safe out there!"

"Actually, I feel very safe. The community is great. Everyone looks out for each other." Maybe she was exaggerating a little, but she didn't want her mother worrying.

"They didn't look out for the guy in the dumpster! The police aren't saying much, but it sounds like he was murdered."

"Every town has crime. After this, things will probably be quiet for a few years. There's no point in being scared."

Adam pulled into a parking lot.

"Mom, I need to get off the phone now."

As soon as Adam turned off his engine, Cassie could hear dogs barking.

"All right, but call me back tonight!"

"If I have time." Cassie did not want to make that call. "I love you."

"You too. Bye."

"Bye." Cassie sighed and unfastened her seatbelt.

"Everything okay?" Adam asked.

"She's just worried. Let's go."

When they walked into the animal shelter's lobby, the sound doubled in volume.

A young woman behind the front desk looked up and smiled. "Hey, Adam. What's up?"

"This is my friend and coworker Cassie. I'd like to show her around."

"Cool. Cassie, I'm Teresa. Let me know if you guys need anything."

"Thank you," Cassie said.

Adam led her down a short hall to the right. "Usually it's an older lady named Agnes who's on duty when I come in. But their shifts rotate, so you never know. Ready for it to get *really* loud?"

Cassie smiled and gave him a nod.

Adam pushed open the door at the end of the hall, and the scattered barking turned into a roar.

Resisting the urge to cover her ears, Cassie widened her eyes at Adam to show that the chorus of barking exceeded her expectations.

Adam grinned in return and led Cassie past several indoor dog runs. The occupants ran forward and reared up to put their front paws against the metal mesh doors. He paused at the cage of a mid-sized tricolor dog and carefully unlatched the door.

The dog put its paws on Adam's legs and looked up at him with large brown eyes.

Cassie entered the run and closed the door behind them. "Who's this?" she asked loudly, to be heard over the barking that had yet to die down.

"Anabelle. She's a sweetie. Her owner passed away, and the family couldn't take her."

"Aw, that's sad." Cassie gave Adam a suspicious look as she reached over to scratch behind the dog's ear. "You picked a beagle mix on purpose, didn't you?"

"Wanna adopt?"

She laughed. "I knew it. Can't adopt right now. Our apartment building has a no-pet policy."

"Too bad."

"Kind of a good thing, because this girl is hard to resist." Cassie stroked the colorful dog's glossy head.

"Care to see the mascot?"

She tilted her head. "Mascot?"

The barking had lessened, so they didn't have to shout to hear each other anymore. Adam led the way, pausing to check that Anabelle's door was secure before they moved away from it. "Boscoe was brought in by animal control. We don't know who he belonged to, or if he was born stray. No one wanted to get close to him until they figured out he's fine with women."

Cassie had met people with male-aggressive dogs before. "So a man probably abused him?"

"Possibly. If we knew exactly what happened, he might be curable, but so far I haven't had any luck with him."

They came to an empty run, and then a yellow-tan shape

darted to the front of the next enclosure with a ferocious bellow. The dog snarled and bit the wire door, his fangs sticking through.

Even though she had known the dog would act aggressively toward Adam, Cassie still jumped, her heart racing.

"Easy, fella." Adam's tone was light, as if the dog had just played a little too rough. "I brought someone to meet you." He stepped back a few paces. "He won't hurt you as long as I'm out of reach. Promise."

As Cassie hesitantly approached, a change came over Boscoe. She saw his half-pricked ears go floppy, his stiff tail wag slowly, and his head move back and forth as he sniffed the air. He looked almost puppyish. "Hello, Boscoe."

The dog licked the mesh of the door, no longer menacing in the slightest. When Cassie put her hand through the gap at the side of the door, it got a friendly lick. Her heart melted.

"Is he adoptable?"

"Not like this. Even if some nice lady took him, she'd have to keep him away from strangers. He wouldn't be much better off than here, and there'd be a danger of him escaping and hurting someone. They said he should probably be put down, but they're hoping for a minor miracle for him."

"That's really sad."

"I know how to cheer you up." Adam motioned for Cassie to follow him.

Their next stop was a warm room with several cat trees and upholstered shelves along the walls. About eight cats of varying colors and hair lengths lounged on the surfaces. Most of them sat up when Adam and Cassie entered.

"Be careful not to let anyone escape."

Cassie closed the door behind them. "Wow, they're so chill."

"Yeah, these are the adult cats who get along well. They get visited all the time by prospective owners. And me." Adam scooped up a tawny, longhaired feline. "Best therapy ever."

"And cheaper than most." Cassie smiled and squatted down

to let a tortoiseshell cat sniff her hand. "Pretty green eyes on this one."

They admired, petted, and held cats for a good twenty minutes before Adam suggested picking up dinner.

"I guess we should." Cassie put down the white cat who had been patting her face with one paw, begging for more attention as she held him. "Bye-bye Jack Frost. Boop." She touched his pink nose with one finger. "Pizza?"

"Sounds good. You like supreme?"

After Adam called in their order, they headed out in his truck.

"So, tomorrow …" Cassie said slowly. "Think we could go to the track?"

Adam sighed. "You're really not going to let that go, are you?"

"Nope."

"Are they open?"

Cassie quickly performed a search on her phone. "First race is at ten."

"Hmm. It's your day off, but I'd have to take time away from work."

Cassie watched Adam's face expectantly.

"Reuben will cover for me for a couple of hours, I'm sure." He changed lanes and made a turn then said slowly, "I guess we can go in the morning. But I want you to promise we'll stay together and not poke into things too much."

"Of course. Well, how much is too much?"

"I'll know it when I see it."

———

Ellsborough racetrack had a one-mile oval track. It saw enough business in the summer to host a couple of minor stakes races. The rest of the card was taken up by handicaps, allowance races, claims races, and maidens.

As an animal lover, Adam usually caught the Kentucky Derby on TV every year, and he knew some of the basic lingo, but that didn't mean he felt at home at the track. He was glad there was no parking or entry fee at Ellsborough. Carrying their own water bottles, they might get through the morning without buying anything other than the racing form he carried.

Cassie tagged along after him, looking at her map of the track and stable area. "Where should we go first?"

He shrugged. "This is your party. Where do you want to go?"

"I should have asked Lucy for some pointers." She stepped closer and lowered her voice. "How does a person meet a bookie?"

"I don't know much more than you do. But I guess we should go where the serious gamblers will go—the railbirds. They'll be hanging around the paddock before the first race."

"That's where they get ready?"

"It's where the horses circle and the jockeys mount up after getting ready in the stable area."

"Hey, you know a lot about this."

"Not really."

"Sure you're not a gambler too?" Cassie's smile looked mischievous.

Adam couldn't help smiling back. He shook his head as he led the way around the track's backstretch. "I'm not. Well, I've made a little bet with a friend before, but I've never paid for a betting slip."

"Hmm. Do you think gambling is a sin?"

"I guess it's like a lot of things. It can definitely be a sin if you let it. But I don't think there's any harm in betting pretend money."

"Oh, that's a fun idea. I'll bet you a hundred fun bucks that I can pick a better horse than yours."

"Sure. I'll accept your IOU."

"You're confident."

The human traffic got thicker as they approached the paddock. Adam wondered if it was all right to reach for Cassie's hand. Then a group of spectators swarmed toward them from the side, and his misgivings disappeared. He grabbed her hand and tugged her forward until they had a little more space.

"Sorry about that. I was afraid we'd get separated."

"You're fine," she said. "I wouldn't want to get lost here." She kept hold of his hand.

With a little nod, Adam continued on. This racecourse wasn't as large as some, but there were several structures around the track besides the grandstand, and the number of people thronging the public areas surprised him.

They managed to carve a path through the crowd milling around the open area next to the paddock. There, Adam finally released Cassie's hand and leaned on the worn metal railing that separated spectators from the contestants.

"All right, who do you like?" Adam had to speak up to be heard over the murmuring crowd.

Cassie looked at the horses being led in a circle. She appeared to focus on each of the racers as they followed their handlers past the rail. Their jockeys came out of the weighing room and waited to one side.

The call *Riders up!* came over the loudspeaker. The jockeys, wearing their stables' colorful silks, went to their horses in turn.

"Look." Cassie nudged his arm. "One of them's a woman!"

Adam watched, noting that the female jockey mounted horse number 4. With the riders in the saddle, the horses walked daintily, some of them prancing a little as they moved around the ring. One snorted and shook its head as it passed them. The competing horses seemed excited for the action to begin.

"Wow, they all look amazing," Cassie said.

Adam glanced around. "Hurry up and pick one. It's almost post time."

"Um …" Her gaze landed on the tall dark bay the woman rode, and she pointed. "That one." The jockey's orange and yellow jacket sported a number 4, as did the blanket showing behind the saddle.

Adam grinned and checked the numbers on his form. "Tampa Dusk. All right. I'll take Mind Your Manners, the chestnut over there."

A bugle sounded, startling Cassie.

"Let's get over to the stands and find a place to watch," Adam said. "They'll be going out on the track now."

"Okay." This time, Cassie reached for Adam's hand first.

Adam's heart sped up. He kept his gaze ahead of them, hoping he didn't look flustered.

They entered the stands on the backstretch. There were plenty of open places, so it didn't take long to find seats. The announcer called out the names and positions of each horse.

"This is the post parade," Adam told Cassie. "If this were the main attraction, they might have band music playing."

She smiled. "And if it were the Kentucky Derby, they'd sing 'My Old Kentucky Home.' Right?"

"Uh-huh."

Each of the thoroughbreds came through the opening, led by another rider on an accompanying horse.

"Why do they all have to have a buddy horse?" Cassie asked.

Adam tried to remember the racecourse terms he'd skimmed on the Internet. "Uh, those are the lead ponies. They give the racers support and help keep them calm before they go to the starting gate."

"Ponies." Cassie frowned, studying the pairs of horses passing by them. "They're not small enough to be ponies, are they?"

Adam shrugged. "That's what they call them. I read it online. Lead ponies or track ponies. Most of them are older horses, and ones that have a quiet disposition."

"I see. I like the Appaloosa that's helping my number four." She turned and smiled up at him. "Last chance to change your pick."

"Nope, I'm good with number seven."

"Lucky number?"

"No such thing." He took her growing smile to mean that she agreed. Cassie seemed to be enjoying herself. Maybe they would just have a pleasant morning and not worry about Lucy's bookie. Besides, the brochure he held said people could use betting machines, too, or even bet online if they subscribed to particular sites. How many people actually used a bookie these days?

The eight horses filed toward the chutes. One lanky chestnut halted and threw his head back. The handler and jockey urged him firmly on, and soon all eight were in place.

"It's not unusual for a horse or two to act claustrophobic at the gate and need a little encouragement." Adam checked the time on his phone. "They'll break any time."

"Oh man, I feel nervous now."

That's cute. He held back a chuckle. Never before had he seen her so excited.

The starting bell sounded, and the horses burst into sight. Many people around them stood to see better, so Adam and Cassie followed suit.

"Who's in front?" Cassie shouted. "Where's number four?"

"I don't know. Seven is trying to find his way to the rail."

They chatted excitedly as the horses strung out along the inner side of the track heading into the first turn. When they came around the backstretch, they saw that Adam's chestnut was running third. Cassie's bay was struggling to hold fifth place.

As the pack rounded the far turn, the bay passed another horse even as a lighter bay competitor zoomed up on his right. Meanwhile, the chestnut managed to settle in second as they entered the homestretch.

"Let's go, Manners!" Adam shouted, surprising himself with his own enthusiasm.

Cassie grabbed his arm and bounced on her toes. "Tampa Dusk! Tampa Dusk!"

But her horse was trailing the field when the sandy bay caught Adam's pick at the finish line.

"Looks like I got third," Adam said.

"I don't even know where my horse finished." Cassie laughed sheepishly. "I guess I owe you a hundred fun bucks." Suddenly, her face fell. She turned toward the track again.

"What is it?" he asked.

"Don't look now, but someone around your five o'clock is watching us."

CHAPTER
THIRTEEN

Cassie stared at the man. She wasn't sure what about him made her feel threatened. He was casually dressed, but he seemed to fit into the scene as though he belonged there. He looked like he was in his forties, and his wavy hair, mustache, and slight slouch told her nothing. It was the eyes. His cold, dark eyes seemed to pierce her, and she shivered.

Adam threw a quick glance over his shoulder then grasped her hand. "Let's go."

He led her swiftly to the stairway, then downward, to the bottom level of the stands. When he turned toward the exit that led to a tunnel beneath the infield and out to the parking lot, Cassie halted in her tracks, forcing him to stop too.

"I thought we'd had enough for one day," Adam said uncertainly.

"But we haven't even looked for Lucy."

He let out a short sigh. "We're supposed to meet with the seniors later, and anyway, I don't think she's here."

"Why not?"

"For one thing, she's probably doing her betting off-track, and for another, she might be scared to show her face here now that her secret's out."

"Possibly," Cassie said, "but she told me she loves coming to watch the races up close. She was very passionate about it, and she didn't say she wouldn't come anymore."

Adam looked back toward the stands they'd left. "Well, whoever that guy is, I don't want him bothering us. Let's at least get on the front side of the track."

They walked swiftly among a moving crowd. Some people headed the way they did, but others were aiming for the backstretch. At last they came up a set of concrete stairs. Cassie looked around in the bright sunlight to orient herself and found they were a long way from the paddock but close to the main grandstand.

"I think there's a café down here a little ways." She pointed in the direction of the track manager's office and the betting windows. "Can we just look in there?" *And maybe scan the lines of bettors waiting to plunk their money down.*

"I guess," Adam said, "but if she's not there, or if we see that guy eyeing us again ..."

"Right." Cassie grabbed his hand and set off.

Outside the café, under the sign reading "Win, Place, or Show," she paused and studied the people several yards away, eagerly waiting to part with their money.

"I don't see Lucy."

"Me either," Adam said. "Come on, let's get a soda."

"Okay."

They stepped into the dim building, and Cassie stopped and squeezed her eyes partway shut.

"This looks more like a bar."

Two to four people sat at most of the small tables dotting the room, with glasses or mugs before them. To the right lay a long counter, where two servers worked. No one seemed to be getting a meal here, just drinks and snacks.

"Looks like we picked the wrong concession." Adam had pulled out his brochure and squinted at the map of the racecourse. "Yeah, the café is the other direction from where we were sitting."

A middle-aged man entered behind them with a ticket in his hand. He tucked it into his shirt pocket as he walked toward the bar.

Cassie gave him a big smile.

"Hi. Got any tips for the next race?"

The man blinked then returned her smile. Eyeing Adam uncertainly, he said, "Well, my money's on Regifted."

"Sweet," Cassie said. "Hey, do you know a guy named Jeff Patterson?"

"I don't think so. Excuse me." The man edged sideways to pass them and walked away.

Adam frowned at her.

"What?" Cassie asked.

"Not very subtle."

She sighed. "How else do we expect to learn anything?"

"I don't know, but we don't want to draw attention to ourselves, do we?"

Thinking that over, she scrunched up her face. "Does it matter?"

Adam looked around the room. "I don't think either of them's in here."

"We should at least ask the bartenders if they knew Jeff."

"I thought you were looking for Lucy."

"Well, I am—or anything about the connection between them."

A man behind Adam stepped closer, and Cassie sucked in a quick breath. It was the dark-eyed man from the backstretch. How long had he been there? *And was he standing close enough to hear me mention Jeff's name and Lucy's?*

Adam's eyebrows drew together as he gazed at her, and suddenly he seemed to catch on. He whirled around, putting him face-to-face with the man who'd watched them earlier.

Before either Adam or Cassie could speak, the dark-eyed man said, "You two should leave."

To Cassie's surprise, Adam squared his shoulders and looked him in the eye. "We'll leave when we want to."

The man stared at him a moment longer then turned abruptly and strode to the bar.

"Come on," Adam whispered. "I think we want to."

She couldn't help but agree. As she turned back toward Adam, an older man passed, headed for the exit. He didn't seem to notice them but ambled on by.

"Hal?" She clutched Adam's arm. "That's Hal Tinley."

"What's he doing here?" Adam seized her hand and pulled her with him. They caught up with Hal just outside the door.

"Hal," Cassie said. "Mr. Tinley!"

He jerked to a stop and turned around. "Wh—oh, *Cassie*? And this is your friend." Hal held out his hand.

"Adam," she said quickly. "Hal, is Lucy with you?"

"No, no." Hal looked surreptitiously over his shoulder. "I only came here to look for her. I saw Lucy drive away this morning, and I thought she might be coming here. But it seems my outing was for naught."

"Why did you think she'd be here?" Adam asked.

Cassie frowned. As far as they knew, Hal was in the dark about Lucy's hobby.

He made a grim face. "Listen, don't let on I told you, okay? I found some betting slips at her place a few days ago. She was in the kitchen fixing us some lemonade, and I went to straighten some magazines on the coffee table, and there they were, tucked underneath. Like she'd tried to hide them quick when I came to the door."

Cassie nodded. "She didn't want you to know, but I told her she should tell you."

Hal's eyes widened. "You knew?" He flicked a glance at Adam. "Both of you?"

"Yeah, she told me a few days ago, and Adam and I

talked to her about it yesterday." Cassie touched his arm. "Hey, we were going to the café—went in that place by mistake." She nodded toward the bar's entrance. "How would you like to walk over to the café with us and get a soda or something?"

"Uh, okay, I guess. You might miss the next race."

"Do you mind if we do?" Adam asked.

"No, not me. I'm not betting on anything."

"Neither are we," Cassie assured him.

The three entered the café together. The next race was about to start, and most racegoers had abandoned the eatery to watch, so they had their pick of tables.

"What do you want?" Adam asked. "My treat."

"It's too early for lunch," Cassie said.

Adam checked his phone. "Not by much. Want a sandwich?"

"Maybe a pastry." Cassie gave him a guilty smile.

"That sounds good," Hal said. "How about doughnuts all around?"

They soon had their coffee and doughnuts. Hal took a big bite of his lemon-filled and chewed with a blissful expression. He swallowed and reached for his mug. "I figured this was Lucy's secret, and I didn't want to ask and upset her."

"We probably shouldn't give you any details," Adam said, "but she did say she's had some losses."

Cassie jumped in. "But she also said the bookie won't let her get in too deep. If she reaches a certain amount, he won't let her bet any more until she's paid up."

Hal's eyebrows shot up. "She's using a bookie?"

"Well, yeah." Cassie wished she'd kept quiet.

"I guess I should have known from the slips I found. A couple of them had handwritten numbers on them." Shaking his head, Hal took another big bite of his rapidly disappearing doughnut.

"I think this whole thing has shaken her," Adam said. "I

don't know Lucy well, but she seemed to be having second thoughts when we talked to her."

"What whole thing?" Hal asked. "The gambling?"

Adam looked apologetically at Cassie. "No, I meant the thing with Jeff Patterson."

Cassie gritted her teeth. They'd told Lucy they wouldn't squeal on her. Now it was all coming out. *But Hal already knew. What else could we do?*

"Hold on. What does Patterson have to do with this?"

"He ..." Adam looked to Cassie with an almost frantic expression, pleading for help.

"We weren't supposed to say anything," Cassie said. "We encouraged Lucy to tell you about it. Jeff was a—a runner, I guess you call it—for her bookie. He came to see her the morning he died."

"Oh, man." Hal grabbed his mug and took a deep drink of his coffee.

CHAPTER
FOURTEEN

"I was worried she might be in over her head, but this is really serious." Hal appeared to be muttering more to himself than to Adam and Cassie. He looked up. "I should look through the stands to make sure she's not here. She could be in actual danger. Don't you think?"

"You could try calling her," Adam suggested, wondering why it hadn't occurred to Hal earlier. "Does she have a house phone?"

"No, just a cell. But I might be able to hear the crowd if she's in the stands. "I'll step into the restroom where it's quieter and try calling. You two want to wait a minute?"

Adam glanced at Cassie, who nodded. "Sure, we'll wait."

They watched Hal cross the dining area and push through the door of the men's room. That side of the café was dim, making the square of light from the glass side door look bright in comparison.

"It's sweet that he's so concerned," Cassie said.

"He has reason to be. However slightly she's involved, a man died, and we're still not sure why."

"I know why." Cassie frowned at her mug. "He was a rotten guy, and someone had enough."

"Well, yeah. We know that much."

Hal came back as Adam was draining the last of his coffee from his cup. The elderly man looked less anxious than he had when he left them.

"She's with Nita at the bead shop," he reported. "I heard Nita's voice too. And nothing that sounded like the track."

"Good," said Cassie. "You might want to tell Lucy that you know about the gambling. It's been hard enough for us to keep it a secret. It has a way of coming out. Lucy told me about it by accident originally."

Hal shifted his weight. "Maybe so. I'll think about it. I should probably run along now."

"Take care," Adam said.

"Right. You too."

Cassie hunched her shoulders, standing with her elbow in one hand and her chin in the other.

"What are you thinking?" Adam asked. He didn't have her figured out yet, but he was sure this posture meant something.

"Oh … I just thought it would be kind of funny if all the folks at Silver Dawn knew all of each other's secrets already but were pretending *not* to know, like Hal with the gambling. It could sure make for a lot of awkward situations."

"Yeah, it would. I think we should go soon too. I still have to—"

He broke off as two men entered the café, talking as they walked. One was their mysterious mustached follower from earlier. The other was a middle-aged man with graying hair and a formidable scowl.

Adam grabbed Cassie's hand and pulled her toward the side door.

Cassie let out a surprised "Hey—" but then followed him without another word.

Once outside, Adam paused as his eyes adjusted to the glaring sun. He turned them toward the track's exit.

"Was that him again?" Cassie asked.

"Yup. I think we should get out of here." He led the way at a brisk walk.

"Did you notice the other guy?"

"Yeah. Dark clothes. Imposing. Like an enforcer. But that's if we let our imaginations run wild."

Adam's eyes landed on another familiar face coming toward them through the crowd, seemingly out of nowhere. "Oh, no."

"What's wrong?"

"It's Mrs. Reuben!" He turned up the collar of his jacket, hoping to obscure his face. "If she sees me, she might mention it to her husband."

"So?"

"What will he think if he knows I took the morning off to go to the track?"

"Isn't that a little silly? I mean, she's here too. Clearly, they don't think the track is all that bad."

Adam managed to keep some strangers between them and their boss's wife as she passed. "Okay, I don't think she noticed."

Cassie chuckled.

"What?"

"Oh, nothing. You looked a little silly, is all."

He didn't know what to say to that. He just hoped that looking silly was more endearing to her than off-putting.

"Thanks for a memorable morning," Adam said as he pulled into her apartment building's lot.

"Yeah, I'll never forget you hiding from the boss's wife." Cassie opened the door and hopped out. She stayed at the apartment just long enough to freshen up. Then she headed straight back to Silver Dawn.

Hal's car was in his driveway. In fact, it looked like everyone was home now, even Nita. Cassie spotted Hal and Gerald standing on Ed and Flossie's patio. She waved and parked in front of the house, then walked toward them.

The closer she got, the more she could see that the two men seemed agitated. Something must be wrong. "What's going on?" she asked them, not sure she wanted to know.

Without the usual pleasantries, Gerald said, "Everyone else is in there." He pointed at Flossie's door. "They came and picked up Ed."

"Who did?"

"The police," said Hal. "Said he needed to answer some questions downtown. Flossie's beside herself."

"Oh, poor Flossie. Should I go in?"

"She'd probably like to see you," said Gerald.

Cassie nodded and went up to the door. Under the circumstances, she decided to let herself in without knocking. She found the ladies of Silver Dawn huddled around Flossie, who sat at one end of her sofa. Nita held a box of tissues where Flossie could reach them.

Flossie, with a tissue already in her hand, looked up at Cassie with red eyes. "Oh, Cassie, dear. Did they tell you what happened? They took Ed away. To the lockup!"

"To the police station," Lucy said gently.

"They think he's a m-murderer!" A fresh tear ran down Flossie's wrinkled cheek.

"I'm sure they haven't made up their minds about it," Cassie said. Since the other ladies were so close around Flossie, she knelt on the floor in front of her. "Hal said they're going to question him."

"Did he tell you they put handcuffs on him?" She sobbed, and Lucy rubbed her back.

"Handcuffs? Really?" It was hard to picture officers restraining a sweet, elderly gentleman as if he were dangerous.

"I know!" Nita shook her head.

Flossie swiped at her tears with the back of her hand. "Ridiculous. But I guess if he objected, they could have said he was 'resisting,' so he did the right thing in cooperating, right Cassie?"

"Yeah, you're right." Cassie felt a pang of guilt. Adam had wanted the group to go to the police with their story last night. Now it seemed like waiting was the wrong call. "I'm so sorry, Flossie. Would you like me to go to the police station and check on him?"

"Would they even let you see him?" Flossie blew her nose before speaking again. "Won't they have him in one of those interrogation rooms with the one-way window and someone yelling at him?" She released another sob.

"I don't know," Cassie admitted. "I don't think they'd yell at him. Ed's not guilty of anything, and I'm sure that will become apparent through talking to him. But it won't hurt anything for me to ask about him, right? I can at least see if the cop I know is there."

Flossie sniffed. "I guess it won't hurt anything at this point."

"Right." Cassie patted Flossie's hand and got up off the floor. "No promises, but I'll see if I can find out anything. You just take it easy. Have some tea. Maybe try to eat something."

"We'll look after her," Lucy promised.

"Okay. I hope I'll be able to tell you something soon."

As she parked at the police station, Cassie thought over what she would say when she went inside. *I'm Cassie Willis, and I'm here for an inmate.* No, that wasn't right! She rehearsed some alternate introductions, but her pulse was still pounding. "Here goes nothing," she muttered to herself.

She tried to at least appear calm as she entered the waiting room and approached the information desk.

The man behind the glass-enclosed desk looked about a decade older than Cassie. He met her eyes and asked, "May I help you?"

"Yes. I'm here for Ed Simonson. I mean ..." Cassie bit her lip. "See, he's a friend, and his wife told me he was brought here for questioning. She's worried, and I wanted to check on him."

"I see. May I have your name, please?"

Cassie spent the next several minutes giving her basic information and watching for any sign of Travis. Finally, she asked, "Is Travis Doake at the station? He's an acquaintance." She nearly said "friend," but worried that the duty officer might reach the conclusion that she was too involved and might create some sort of conflict of interest.

"I can check. In the meantime, you can have a seat. I'll let you know if I have any information for you."

"Okay. Thank you." Disappointed that she hadn't learned anything and a little embarrassed for trying, Cassie chose a seat between two empty ones and hoped no one would sit next to her. There was no telling the kind of people who showed up at police stations in the middle of the day.

She scrolled on her phone a bit and tried not to listen to the next person who approached the desk for information. Ignoring the individual became difficult when she ascertained that it was a woman worried about a family member who wasn't responding to her phone. The woman was becoming louder and more agitated by the minute.

Cassie moved away and took out her phone. She needed some support, Jenna was at work. She hesitated then called Adam's desk phone, hoping to avoid interrupting work calls with his ringing cell.

"Reuben's Rubbish Removal."

"Adam?"

"Cassie?"

She smiled, relieved to hear his voice. "Hi. If you're busy, I can call later."

"No, you caught me at a good time. What's up?"

"Oh ... I'm at the police station." After a heavy pause, Cassie added, "I'm not in trouble."

"Okay. Why are you there?"

She explained what had happened at Silver Dawn and that she had hoped to get some news for Flossie.

"I know you want to help, but you're probably just going to sit there all day. I doubt they'll let you see him before they're done interviewing him."

"Yeah … but at least he'll see a friendly face when he gets out. And I can drive him home."

"I'm sure he'd appreciate that, but are you sure you want to wait on him?"

"I feel kind of guilty for not siding with you last night. If …" Cassie glanced around, not sure how far her voice carried in the mostly empty room. "You know, things might have been different."

"We can't do anything about that now. Are you okay? Is there anything I can do for you while you wait?"

"Nothing I can think of."

The duty officer caught Cassie's eye and beckoned to her.

She got to her feet. "Thanks for asking, though."

"No problem. Let me know if anything comes up. And when you're headed out of there."

"All right. Bye."

"Bye."

She shoved her phone in her pocket as she approached the desk.

"Miss Willis, Officer Doake is away from the station right now."

"All right. Thanks for checking."

He nodded. "And Mister Simonson is here for questioning. That's all I can tell you right now."

"Has he been charged with anything?"

"I can't discuss that at this time."

"I see. I guess I'll just wait until they finish."

She went back to her seat and unlocked her phone again. She checked her messages and sent Flossie a text saying, "Still in

125

questioning. I'm waiting for him." She used half of her battery life on an app game before the duty officer called her name from the desk.

"Mister Simonson is being released."

Even though she had told herself many times that everything would be all right, Cassie felt immense relief. "Thank you."

"He'll come through that door there." He pointed across the waiting room.

Cassie gave him a smile. "Thank you so much."

Before long, another officer opened the door, and Ed came through it. He looked tired until his eyes fell on Cassie—then his fatigue was masked by surprise.

"Cassie? What are you doing here?"

She put on her best confident smile. "I'm here to escort you home, Ed. Got your two dollars and your change of clothes?"

"What?"

"Sorry, that was a joke about the way they used to release prisoners way back when." She patted his shoulder. "You ready to go?"

"I sure am. Thanks for coming to get me."

Cassie decided to keep her long wait to herself. "No problem. Everyone's worried about you. Do you have your phone?"

"Yeah, they gave it back. I'll call Flossie and let her know we're coming."

"Good. I'll text Adam."

When Cassie pulled back into the cul-de-sac at Silver Dawn, everything was quiet.

"Lucy's got a visitor." Ed nodded toward Lucy's house.

Cassie saw a sleek black sedan parked behind Lucy's car in her driveway. "I wonder who it is."

"It's not her niece, unless she's in a new car. I don't recognize it."

"Hmm."

They walked up Ed's driveway together, and he opened the door for her.

Ed and Flossie's other neighbors were all assembled in the living room.

Flossie jumped up with surprising energy for someone of her age. She rushed into Ed's arms and he held her close. "Are you all right, honey?"

"I'm fine." He patted her back. "No damage."

Hal spoke up. "We've been talking about coming clean."

CHAPTER
FIFTEEN

"I think that's a good idea." Cassie looked around at the group of seniors. "Be up front with the police about what happened here."

Ed's mouth skewed. "I don't know. What will happen then? Are they going to take everybody in and treat us all like criminals, instead of just me?"

Cassie found a seat in one of the armchairs and considered their woeful faces. Nobody spoke, waiting to hear her opinion. She didn't want to give them bad advice and land them all in hot water, but she truly felt that continuing to hold back would hurt them more in the long run. She sent up a quick silent prayer for wisdom and took a deep breath.

"Okay. You want to know what I think. Well, here it is. I think getting it out in the open is the best thing you can do. You can support each other, but you need to be truthful. If even one person tries to avoid telling something about this whole mess, it will make all of you look bad."

"She's right," Hal said firmly. "No more of this pussyfooting around. Let's get 'er done."

"I agree," Nita said.

Flossie looked at Ed, and he shrugged.

"Ed, I'm sorry they treated you the way they did," Cassie said. "I know you want to protect Flossie and the others. But right now, the best way to do that is probably by letting everyone tell the truth."

He sighed. "I suppose so."

"I'll go get Lucy," Hal said, stepping toward the door.

Cassie turned toward him. "There was someone at her house, remember?"

Hal hesitated and looked around. "Yeah. Anyone know whose car that is in her driveway?"

The others looked at each other and shook their heads.

"She went home about an hour after you left," Nita said.

Flossie nodded. "She said she wanted to do a little cleaning this afternoon."

Gerald leaned forward. "I looked out the window about ten minutes ago, and I saw a big, black car drive in. Hal and I went outside, but by the time we got out front, whoever was in it was gone—into the house, we figured."

Remembering the odd events at the racetrack that morning, Cassie made a quick decision. "Okay, Hal, I'm coming with you."

"All right. We'll be right back," Hal said to his friends. He opened the door for Cassie and followed her outside. "You don't think Lucy's in trouble, do you?"

"I certainly hope not, but there's safety in numbers. If there's no problem, she won't care that we're both on her doorstep."

"And if there is ..."

Cassie swallowed hard. "We'll have to play it by ear."

They headed across the street toward Lucy's neat little house.

"I sure don't know anyone with a car like that." Hal frowned at the vehicle.

Cassie squinted at the logo on the trunk. "Is that a Cadillac?"

"No, it's a Rolls Royce."

"Oh. Wow. None of *my* friends could afford a car like that."

Hal scowled. "Mine either. What if they're not friends? I should have come over here sooner."

They'd reached Lucy's driveway, and Cassie paused. "Maybe we should have a plan?"

"I just want to get in there and make sure she's okay."

She glanced toward the large living room window and caught a flicker of movement. "Let me try to get underneath that window without them seeing me. I might be able to hear something."

"You don't think we should just ring the bell?"

"Hold on," she said.

He took cover behind a syringa bush, and Cassie ducked low and skittered along the side of the house. When she was beneath the large window, she halted and crouched, trying to calm her heartbeat.

Someone was definitely talking inside the living room. The voice sounded like the low rumble she heard when she emptied her garbage truck's main bay.

A high-pitched voice she recognized as Lucy's—Lucy's when she was in distress—leaped at her through the glass.

"No! You can't do that. I told you I'll get you the money by next week."

"Shut up," came a distinct male voice.

"You've said that for weeks now," said Rumble-Voice.

"I know, but I had a setback. I promise I'll—"

Smack!

Cassie jumped, her heart in her throat. She hurried, hunched over, back to the bush where Hal was hiding.

"I think they hit Lucy," she whispered.

"No! I'm going in."

"You can't just—"

"I'm going. You call the cops."

Hal strode up onto the porch, toward the front door, and Cassie fumbled to get her phone out of her pocket. She clicked the side button to bring it to life. Just as she was about to press the emergency number's call icon, the phone rang. She gulped and looked toward Hal, who stabbed the doorbell with his index finger.

The rumbling voice stopped.

Cassie glanced at her phone's screen. *Adam!* She swiped it and clamped it to her ear.

"Adam! Help!"

"What? What's going on?"

"I'm at Lucy's with Hal, and there are some men in there. They're yelling at her, and I think they hit her."

"Is it the bookie's men?"

"I don't know. I couldn't see them, but I heard their voices. They're bad men. I was going to call 911."

"Okay, you stay put, and I'll call the cops."

She heard the door yanked open and edged back behind the bush so that whoever opened it wouldn't see her.

"Hey," Hal said gruffly. "I'm here to see Lucy."

"Who are you?"

"I'm Hal Tinley. I'm Lucy's neighbor."

"So what do you want?"

"I told you—I want to see Lucy."

"She's busy."

"Oh, I'm sure she'd want to see me anyhow."

"I'll tell her you were here."

"No, I need to see her now." Hal's voice rose insistently.

After a brief pause, the man said, "Okay, come on in, then."

Cassie held her breath. Hal was actually going inside with those two brutes. She could understand his need to assure himself that Lucy was all right, but still. It might be better to wait for the police to arrive.

She hesitated then duck-walked back to her former post under the window.

"What'd you let him in for?" Rumble-Voice spoke so loudly now that she could understand him. He probably stood just inside the window.

The second man, whom Cassie judged to be younger, said, "He wouldn't go away."

Rumble swore. "Are you an idiot?"

Hal spoke up. "Here now. What's all the fuss about? I just want to see Lucy for a minute."

"What about?" came Rumble-Voice's demand.

"Something that's important to her."

"You a wise guy?"

"No, no," Hal said with forced affability. "Where is she, anyway?"

"Sit down over there."

Cassie slowly edged up to where she could barely see over the edge of the window frame. She caught her breath and ducked down again. One man held a pistol, and he was pointing it at Hal. That man was one of the two they'd seen hanging around Ellsborough Racetrack. Rumble-Voice. She pulled in a shaky breath and tapped her phone.

"Adam?" Relief filled her when he answered, and she leaned back against the siding.

"Yeah, Cassie. I'm almost there."

"You are?"

"Yes. I figured I might be closer than the police, so I called them on the desk phone and jumped in the car. I'll be there in five minutes."

"Good, because Hal went inside," she whispered hoarsely. "It's one of those guys from the racetrack, and he has a gun."

"A gun?"

"Yes. Adam, I'm scared. I ducked down so they couldn't see me out the window, but I don't know what they've done with Lucy. I didn't see her inside, but I know she was there a couple minutes ago."

"Hold on. I'll be right there. Don't do anything yet."

"I—Okay." Cassie pulled in a breath. "Adam, what if they hurt Hal?"

"Pray, Cassie. You can't stop them yourself. Just wait and pray."

"Right." She was about to ask if he would keep their call open, but the connection was already gone.

She sneaked back to the bush beside the porch. Above and to her right, the house's door opened. Cassie froze for an instant then tried to make herself smaller. Hunkered down between the steps and the bush, she kept still and dropped her chin onto her chest. If Hal emerged and came down the steps, she'd see him and all would be well. But if someone else came out ...

The footsteps on the porch were firm and brisk. Not like Hal. The younger man, Mr. Mustache, strode onto the driveway and walked toward the Rolls Royce. Cassie's heart pounded. What would she do when he got in and was facing her? Maybe he'd be preoccupied with backing out onto the street and wouldn't notice her.

He'd just reached the front of his vehicle when her phone pinged with an incoming text. Cassie froze, but the man kept walking, apparently not hearing it.

Mr. Mustache strode to his car door and reached for the handle. He looked back toward the house as he opened the door. His gaze landed on her and he frowned. "And who are you?"

Cassie tried to answer, but nothing came out.

He closed the ten yards between them and stood over her scowling.

"Get up," he barked.

Her legs were cramped anyway, and she was glad to change position, but standing eye to eye with the man didn't lessen her fright. Her knees felt wobbly and her throat ached.

He lifted his chin slightly, and she was sure he recognized her. "What are you doing here?"

"I ... I ..." Cassie took courage. "I'm Lucy's friend."

His eyes tightened. "I've seen you before."

"Oh? I guess it's possible." She managed to sound coherent at last, but her voice cracked a little on the last word. "Have you

134

been here before?" She focused on his plentiful mustache. Definitely the man she and Adam had seen at the track. If she could just stall him for four minutes.

Adam drove as fast as he dared on the busy streets. Finally, he turned in at the gates of the Silver Dawn community. There was Kieran, out using the Weedwacker on the grass edging the sidewalk. He squinted forward, trying to pick out Lucy's house. That was hers with the big black Rolls sitting out front.

He hit the brakes just as he came even with Kieran. Maybe the young man could be useful for once. Adam lowered his window.

"Hey, Kieran!"

He paid no attention, and Adam noticed his earbuds. Gritting his teeth, Adam pulled his truck forward a couple of yards, to where Kieran could hardly fail to notice him. Kieran jerked his head up and stared for a moment then shut off the Weedwacker.

"Adam, right? Cassie's friend?" Kieran pulled his earbuds out.

"Yeah. Have you seen Cassie?"

"Nope, not lately, but her car's at Ed Simonson's house."

"Right." Adam's mind whirled as he focused on the other side of the cul-de-sac and spotted Cassie's gray Focus. "Listen, can you do me a favor?"

Kieran looked at the same time doubtful and hopeful, as though he wanted the cool kids to include him in their games but wasn't certain he could hold up his end.

"Like what?"

"Get your karaoke machine."

Kieran's eyes brightened, and his whole face lit up. "Seriously?"

"Yeah. You've got a sound effects disk, don't you?"

"I sure do."

"Bring that."

Kieran laid down the Weedwacker and took off across the nearest lawn. Adam wondered where the manager's family lived. A maintenance shed sat back from the road between two of the houses, but Kieran didn't stop there. His dad's house must be within a street or two, Adam surmised. That, or Kieran had left the machine in his vehicle nearby.

Adam rolled his truck around the curve and pulled over two houses from Lucy's. He got out and approached cautiously. Nobody was outside, and the drapes in the living room picture window were closed. Cassie had said she ducked below the window, and she knew one man had a gun. Someone must have pulled the curtains after that. And where was Cassie now?

He fingered his phone in his pocket. Nope. He couldn't call her. If she was hiding from the men, an incoming call might give her away.

"Adam!"

He whirled around. Kieran ran across the lawns, awkwardly carrying the karaoke machine. Adam held a finger to his lips. Kieran crossed the street and puffed toward him.

Adam met him at the bottom of the porch steps.

"Is there a siren sound effect?"

"Yeah."

"Do it now. Quick as you can."

Kieran stared at him for a second, gulped and knelt to work on the apparatus.

"Here goes."

A moment later, a convincing siren blasted through the air. Across the street and over one house, senior citizens poured out the Simonsons' front door. Adam waved frantically at them, then held up both hands and made pushing motions. He hoped they'd interpret that to mean they should stay put.

Gerald seemed to catch on first. He grabbed Nita's arm and pulled her back toward the door. With Ed and Flossie, the two immediately engaged in a spirited conversation, of which Adam couldn't make out a word.

He leaned closer to Kieran and yelled, "That's enough."

Kieran hit the switch, and the siren stopped. The quiet hung ominously in the air.

Adam strode up the steps and poked Lucy's doorbell. Where were those cops?

"Open up," he called. He didn't dare say *police*, or someone might say he'd falsely claimed to be an officer.

He pounded on the door with his fist. "Open up!"

From inside, a faint noise reached him.

Kieran stepped up beside him. "You want me to—"

Adam held up a hand. "Shh!"

They both put their heads against the door panel and listened.

A feeble wail sounded from inside. Then he heard it plainly.

"Help me!"

"That's Lucy," Kieran said.

Adam seized the doorknob and turned it. The door opened at his touch, and he hurried inside, Kieran following.

"Miss Jansen?" he called. "Lucy? Cassie? Where are you?"

"Here," came a man's voice, and he followed the sound into a small but neat kitchen. Lucy Jansen sat tied to a chair before the table. Hal was kneeling beside her, tugging at the bindings, which looked like clothesline. A dish towel sagged around Lucy's chin. A gag? A red spot showed through Hal's thinning hair.

Adam dashed to Lucy's other side and helped with the rope. "We got you, Lucy."

"Thank you," she gasped.

"You okay, Hal? Where's Cassie?" Adam asked.

Lucy looked up at him with faded blue eyes. "They took her. After they slugged Hal, those men took her out the back."

CHAPTER
SIXTEEN

Adam rushed to the window in time to see the Rolls Royce disappearing toward the community's gateway. Could he follow them?

"Should I call the police?" Kieran asked.

"They're already on their way." Adam got out his phone and found Cassie's number. "Make sure Hal's head is all right."

"They were trying to knock me out," said Hal. "I wasn't gonna hold still for that! He got me, but not hard enough."

"You were so brave," Lucy told him.

Adam waited through several rings. He hoped and prayed that Cassie had shaken the men off and could answer him, but there was always the possibility that she had lost her phone along the way. The ringing stopped.

He pulled his cell away from his ear to look at it. The call had connected, but no one was talking. He lifted the phone again and spoke softly. "Cassie?"

"Who's this?" asked a man's deep voice.

Adam's heart jumped into overdrive. He moved to the sitting room, away from the others. Somehow, he had the presence of mind to neither impersonate a police officer nor to give his real name. "You can call me Mac."

"Friend of Cassie, I take it."

"You don't have to hurt her. And you'll be in a lot more trouble if you do."

"Listen, hero. I'm not stupid. You're not telling me anything I don't know. Those sirens weren't real, were they? But the real cops are on their way, and they'll have an APB on my car in no time. I want some insurance that they're not going to get a description of it. You care about this chick. So, I'll just keep her until the fuss dies down. When I'm sure you and those old-timers didn't squeal on me, I'll let her go. Not before."

Adam had seen enough crime shows to know that the more time that passed, the less likely kidnappers were to return their victims. He couldn't leave Cassie with those men. *Keep me calm, Lord.* He tried to tamp down his fears. "I can do better than that. I'll be your hostage. I imagine she's pretty scared by now. She's not going to tell the police anything. You can keep me until you're satisfied of that. I live alone. I won't be missed. But she has a roommate."

There was a long pause, which Adam took as a sign that his offer was being considered.

"How do I know the cops aren't there now, listening?"

"You can't know for sure, but I understand that if I don't come alone, it won't be good for Cassie. I promise I won't tell a soul where I'm going."

"You don't have to, if they just overhear where I tell you to meet up."

Adam thought he heard Cassie's voice in the background, but he couldn't make out what she said.

The man spoke again, sounding slightly different. "You're on speaker, Mac. Your girl says she knows where we can meet."

"Mac?" Cassie's voice was clear now.

"Hey," he answered, trying not to sound worried. "Are you okay?"

"Yeah. I was just thinking—we could meet up at Boscoe's. No one knows where that is, right?"

The only Boscoe Adam knew was the animal shelter mascot. "Yeah, you're right. And no one's there after six or so. I can get there in fifteen minutes and leave it unlocked for you. That way, you can stay inside until someone can come pick you up."

There were some scuffling sounds, and then the man spoke again. "All right, get moving. Cassie here is going to give us directions as we go. And you're right—it won't go well for her if you don't come alone."

The call ended. Adam stared at the phone in his shaking hand.

"Who was that?" Kieran stood in the doorway.

Adam looked up at him, doubt flooding his mind. He reached for his faith and clung to it. "Kieran, I need your help again."

"Uh … sure. What's up?"

Adam walked over to him so he could speak quietly without the couple in the kitchen overhearing. "I don't want you to lie to the police, but I want you to kind of … forget I was here for a while. Me and Cassie. Just delay telling our part of things for a good twenty minutes or as long as you can, up till then. I need to go do something *right now,* and I can't have them telling me not to leave or sending people to look for me. Talk like you and Hal saved Lucy on your own, and get them to do the same. Can you do that?"

Kieran looked doubtful. "Will it help Cassie?"

"I think so. A lot."

"Okay, I'll try."

Adam slapped him on the shoulder. "It's up to you. I have to go."

Without a backward glance, he hurried out the door and sprinted to his truck.

By the time he was halfway through the neighborhood, Adam could hear sirens. He turned off into another cul-de-sac and waited for the pair of squad cars to pass. Then he circled back and drove out of Silver Dawn, heading for the animal shelter.

Mr. Mustache drove while Cassie directed him from the front passenger seat. Mr. Rumble sat behind her with his gun pointed at her.

"You really don't need to keep pointing that at me," Cassie said. "I'm cooperating."

"Which way next?" Rumble asked.

"Left at the next light."

Cassie's heart pounded uncontrollably. It was exhausting, not knowing what would happen to her. She prayed between directions, asking for safety for both herself and Adam. She felt guilty that he had offered to take her place, but she wasn't giving up on both of them escaping. She had an idea how they might do that, but it would be tricky.

At last, she pointed out the sign for the animal shelter. "That's it."

"It's a pound?" said Mustache. "Who's Boscoe?" He pulled up at the gate and got out to push it open.

"Close it behind us too," Rumble instructed. "Everything needs to look normal."

When they were through the gate and it was shut, Mustache parked next to Adam's forest green Dodge Ram, the only other vehicle in the parking lot. "Hey ... there's no one in that truck."

Cassie waited, feeling lightheaded.

"Where is he?" Rumble demanded.

She took a sharp breath. "He—he said he'd unlock the place for us. He's probably inside."

"I don't like this," said Mustache. "We're real close to the road."

"All right, everyone out," Rumble ordered. "And keep in mind, missy, my gun will be in my pocket. I don't like to ruin a nice jacket, but I can shoot you without taking it out if I have to. So don't try anything."

Cassie swallowed thickly. "I understand."

She got out of the vehicle and walked across the parking lot between her captors. The sound of barking dogs filled the evening air. When they were about halfway to the front door, Adam opened it.

It was good to see him, even in these circumstances. *Maybe everything will be okay. Please protect us, Father.*

"There you are." Rumble's voice had a dangerous edge. "Turn around. Let me see you're unarmed."

Adam put his hands out and turned in a circle.

Cassie heard cars passing, but she didn't dare look back to see if anyone showed signs of suspicion. The drivers were probably too busy rushing home or thinking about going to dinner to notice anything weird happening at the local shelter.

"All right, she's gonna walk toward you, and you pass in the middle. Nice and slow. Either of you does something funny, I'm going to get trigger-happy."

Adam nodded.

Cassie felt like her legs had suddenly gotten heavy. She took a step, and Adam did the same. Somehow, she took another and another. For some reason, it seemed like Adam's steps were tiny. She met his eyes. He was looking at her intently.

When they were close enough, Adam said softly, "Boscoe's waiting just outside the lobby. Let him out."

This was better than Cassie had hoped. She had thought she would have to go all the way back to Boscoe's cage to get him, and by then Adam might be gone. How had he gotten the dog so far through the building? Had it chased him all the way? However he had managed it, the plan was dangerous.

"Are you sure? He doesn't like you either."

"I'll take that chance." Adam reached out to grasp her hand for a moment.

"Come on, keep moving," Rumble barked.

They were closer to the building than to the thugs, and Cassie realized that Adam's small steps had been strategic. She lengthened her own stride, and soon the door was within reach. She heard someone say something behind her, but she focused on getting through the glass door.

Once inside, Cassie rushed across the lobby. She could hear claws scratching on the door to the dog kennel section.

"It's okay, Boscoe," she called. "Good boy."

The scratching stopped and she opened the door. The big yellow dog bounded through, gave her a sniff, and then ran for the front door, snarling.

Cassie followed him. She could see that Adam and the two other men were almost back to the Rolls Royce. "Please don't hurt Adam," she whispered as she pushed the front door open.

"Gentlemen, this is Boscoe," she muttered as the dog charged across the pavement with thunderous barks.

Adam darted to the side, and Boscoe altered his trajectory, following the movement.

Rumble fired a shot at Adam as he vaulted into his truck bed.

Cassie stifled a scream. She couldn't tell if Adam had been hit.

Boscoe changed direction again, stretching out as he sped right at Rumble. The villain pointed his gun at the dog, but he was too late. Boscoe was already sailing at him through the air. The dog's jaws clenched around Rumble's hand, gun and all.

Cassie had never heard a man scream, but now the air was full of the sound—that and cursing. Rumble and Mustache both tried to fight Boscoe off, but his low center of gravity and face full of ivory knives were too much for them. The best they could do was fight their way to a side door and dive into the car, desperately pulling the door shut after them.

Boscoe put his paws on the side of the car and barked menacingly. Then he got back on all fours and trailed over to an object on the ground. He picked it up and wildly shook it back and forth.

Cassie gasped. It was the gun.

CHAPTER
SEVENTEEN

"Boscoe! Easy, boy. Calm down." Cassie's voice kept a quiet tone, but Adam thought it quavered a little. He risked a peek. Boscoe leaped up against the rear passenger door of the kidnappers' car, where the man who had driven cowered below the bottom of the window. The yellowish-tan dog still held the gun in his jaws but growled menacingly and pawed at the window. Cassie moved hesitantly toward Boscoe.

The second man was yelling at the driver, but Adam couldn't hear what he was saying. Mr. Mustache finally seemed to understand what the boss wanted, and as far as he could tell, the man who'd sat in the back seat was the boss. Mustache clambered awkwardly between the two front seats, over the console, and into his place behind the wheel.

Adam edged his face higher above the side of his truck bed in an effort to see better, but Boscoe immediately barked, dropping the gun, and lunged toward him. Adam dove down below the side. Boscoe hesitated then scooted away. When Adam heard his steps retreating, he sneaked another look. Boscoe ran back toward Cassie and stood with one foot on the handgun.

While the dog was momentarily distracted, Mustache started the car's engine. Adam eased up just enough to look toward the gate they'd closed when they came in. If one of the men got out to open that, Boscoe would take him down in seconds. His heart hammered. He didn't want the criminals to get away, but he also didn't want their lives to be at risk. If Boscoe went further than defending him and Cassie, the officials might insist that he be put down.

The dog barked ferociously and jumped up against the car window, his claws scrabbling on the door.

That's it, Adam thought. Scratch the paint, and the police will be able to find that car easier later.

Cassie stood back, white-faced, seemingly frozen to the pavement. Adam wished he could stand beside her, or better yet, pull her into the building. But not with Boscoe on the rampage.

The mustached man threw the transmission in gear and did an impressive tight turn with the Rolls Royce. Adam's throat tightened. Was he going to try to run down Boscoe? The car jerked around and headed straight for the gate they'd shut when they arrived.

Adam started to climb over the side of the truck bed, but Boscoe growled fiercely at him, and he quickly pulled his leg back in.

The car didn't slow down as it approached the gate. Instead, the driver seemed to hit the gas pedal hard. Adam watched in disbelief as the Rolls smashed through the barrier, leaving a mangled mess of metal rods dangling from the hinges. If Boscoe's claws hadn't left a mark on the paint job, the gate surely had.

Boscoe barked and tore to the end of the driveway.

"Come back, fella," Cassie called. To Adam's amazement, the big dog stopped by the broken gate. He barked a few more times then turned back.

"Get the gun," Adam yelled.

Cassie jerked her head in his direction him then whipped around. She ran toward where the dog had dropped the pistol, but Boscoe beat her to the prize. He picked it up and trotted determinedly to Adam's truck, snarling deep in his throat.

"Are you okay?" Cassie called.

"Yeah."

"Do you have your phone?"

He shook his head. "They took it."

"Mine too."

"Go inside and call the police," Adam told her.

Cassie shook her head. "I have to settle Boscoe down. I can't leave you out here with him loose."

"Right." Adam swallowed hard, considering his options. "Look, you keep him occupied, and I'll try to get inside and call them."

She nodded.

"But be careful," he added.

Even though Boscoe had shown Cassie some partiality before, Adam didn't quite trust the big dog not to hurt her now, especially if he felt she was trying to get something away from him. And his teeth might somehow make the gun fire. He was worried for her safety, but what else could they do?

"Hey, Boscoe. Come on, big fella!" Cassie spoke chirpily to Boscoe and took baby steps forward. The mutt actually let her pat his head and neck. She sneaked a quick look at Adam. He gritted his teeth. With Boscoe turned away from him, he sent up a quick silent prayer, easing cautiously over the side of the truck bed by the rear wheel and to the ground.

As he moved quietly toward the door of the building, Cassie continued gingerly patting the dog. She reached behind Boscoe's ear and scratched. Adam turned and hurried to the door, hoping she could keep Boscoe's attention away from his escape. At least the gun's barrel was pointed to the other side, away from her.

He opened the door and looked back. Boscoe now sat in front of Cassie, his big eyes watching her face. She bent lower, and Adam wondered if that was wise. He held his breath as she took a gentle hold on the scruff of Boscoe's neck. The shelter didn't put collars on most of their animals, and Adam wished now they had a different policy. Would Boscoe let her take the gun out of his mouth now? Maybe she wouldn't dare try. He'd better hurry.

On the desk phone, he called 911 and rapidly told the dispatcher where he and Cassie were, saying they needed help. Apparently the woman recognized Cassie's name immediately as the young woman who'd been reported as a kidnap victim half an hour earlier.

"You should stay on the line," the dispatcher said.

"I can't. Sorry. I need to stay with Cassie until the officers get here. But I won't leave this location." He hung up and hurried outside.

Cassie glanced toward him when he opened the door. Adam ducked back and held the door partway open, with a gap of about a foot. When he poked his head outside, Boscoe immediately snarled but still held the gun. Saliva dripped from his jaw.

Adam shielded himself behind the door. "They're coming."

"Can you get a leash?" Cassie called.

"Yeah, but stay clear of that gun barrel."

"I am. Just hurry."

He ducked back into the lobby and grabbed a leash with a slip lead from the rack near the door. A small bag caught his eye, and he grabbed it and tore it open.

He opened the door softly and bent to lay the leash and a bacon-flavored dog treat on the step outside.

"Easy, boy." Cassie continued to stroke Boscoe's head and neck.

"That's his favorite bacon-flavored treat," Adam said.

"Okay, good. Shut the door."

As she turned back to face Boscoe, the dog lowered his head and meekly laid the pistol at her feet. Adam let out a deep sigh and let the door close.

Cassie was smiling now. She renewed her patting and

scratching around Boscoe's ears and talking enthusiastically, though Adam couldn't make out her words. Boscoe pressed his head against her hand, with his ears finally cocked back in a sign of submission, signaling his approval. Adam wished he could place the leash in her hand. *Lord, guide Cassie. Let us get out of this without anyone getting hurt.*

He watched through the glass as she tightened her grasp on the dog's scruff and tugged gently. Boscoe let out a little bark and maintained his position, seated before her, with his head extending over the gun.

Adam could almost feel Cassie's frustration. *He's guarding it.* Now what could she do?

She tried once more to get him to walk with her, standing straight and facing the shelter door. "Heel, Boscoe."

He looked up at her almost mournfully but didn't move.

Okay, Lord, help her! If there's something I can do, show me!

Adam eased the door open a crack.

"Good boy." Giving Boscoe a couple more pats on the head, Cassie pulled in a deep breath. "Stay. You stay here. I'll be right back."

Hesitantly, she left him and walked calmly but swiftly toward the door. Adam kept his eye on the dog.

"Good job," he said softly when she approached the doorstep. "That's a slip lead. Have you used one before?"

She shook her head.

"Get his front leg through the loop and he'll be easier to handle." Boscoe was right where she'd left him, eyeing her quizzically. Adam stood stock still to one side, hoping the dog couldn't see him. When he was sure Cassie's shape shielded him from Boscoe's view, he gave her a thumbs-up, and she grinned. Slowly, she stooped and picked up the leash and the dog treat.

Adam feared Boscoe would take off and run through the smashed gate, but as Cassie approached him he kept his post, guarding the gun. Adam could tell when he'd spotted the leash

—he leaned his head away like a toddler avoiding a spoonful of food.

"Easy, Boscoe. It's okay." Cassie paused between steps but kept speaking to him in a soothing tone as she made her way toward him. How could she stay so calm? Somehow, she managed to keep up the reassuring chatter. At last she was close enough to reach out to Boscoe. He sniffed her hand and accepted the treat. She smiled. "Good boy. Isn't it yummy?"

He allowed her to stroke his head then, and Adam exhaled. *Thank You, Lord!*

Cassie draped the slip lead around the big dog's shoulders and bent to guide one paw through it as Adam had instructed. Adam couldn't hear a sound as she let his paw back down. *He must know what's coming. She must be scared silly.* But Cassie kept patting Boscoe with one hand, holding the leash with the other.

"Come on, boy." She tugged him toward the shelter, and this time he let her guide him and left the gun lying on the pavement in the parking area. They'd almost reached the door when Adam caught the faint wail of a siren.

He opened the door a couple of inches and dropped another treat onto the step. Cassie smiled and picked it up.

"Look, Boscoe. More yummy!"

He took it eagerly from her hand and licked her fingers.

Adam backed away from the door so they could give him a wide berth when they entered the building.

Cassie pushed the door open enough to get Boscoe through it and stepped inside. "Can you take him?"

"I doubt it."

Boscoe growled, his ears pricked toward Adam.

"Nope," Adam said, stepping behind the end of the front desk. "You'd better take him to his cage. Here's another treat." He shook two more from the bag and handed them to her over the countertop.

"Okay, but you go out and get the gun, or at least point it out to the cops."

The siren was louder now. Adam walked around the desk as Cassie guided Boscoe around it so he would not be in the dog's line of sight.

"I'll go out there as soon as you're through the door," Adam said.

Chewing his treat, Boscoe threw a suspicious look in the direction of Adam's voice. Cassie tugged gently on the leash, tightening it up under the dog's armpit. At her coaxing, he quietly accompanied her past the desk and through the door to the kennel area.

Adam ran across the parking area. The ear-piercing siren made him cringe. He stooped toward the pistol but then thought better of touching it. The police would probably prefer that he didn't add his fingerprints to any other marks on it. He stood squarely over it, so the driver wouldn't inadvertently drive over it.

The police car turned into the lot, and the driver did a quick swerve to avoid part of the fallen gate. Adam waited until it halted a few yards from him and two officers climbed out.

"The men who kidnapped Cassie Willis went that way in a black Rolls Royce." Adam pointed down the street to the right of the gate.

"They have Miss Willis?" said the nearest policeman, whose nametag read *D. Healy*.

"No, no. She's safe now. She went inside to put the dog in his cage."

The officer frowned. "Dog? What dog?"

Adam could see that it would take him a minute to explain what had happened. "Did you see Lucy Jansen?" he asked.

"Yes."

"Well, the men who tied her up and threatened her and then hit Hal Tinley are the same men who grabbed Cassie Willis and brought her here. But they left in a hurry and smashed the gate. They went thatta way." He pointed again.

The officer looked at his partner. "Call it in. Our backup may be able to intercept them." He turned back to Adam as the second cop stepped away to make the call on his radio.

"Who are you?"

"I'm Adam MacAllister. I went to help Lucy Jansen with Kieran Harmon. Did you see him?"

"Yes, but he didn't say anything about you."

"I was with him, but when Lucy and Hal told us those men took Cassie, I called her cell phone. One of the kidnappers answered. I offered to take Cassie's place, and to meet them here."

Officer Healy scowled, and Adam almost expected him to growl like Boscoe.

"None of them said anything about that."

"I didn't tell Kieran and the others where I was going. I knew they'd try to stop me." Adam glanced toward the shelter's front door. He was uneasy that Cassie was taking so long.

"Miss Jansen said they were trying to extort money from her."

"That's right. And then Cassie and Hal went to check on Lucy, and those men got the upper hand, so to speak."

The second officer stepped up beside his partner. "The backup and another car are in pursuit of the Rolls."

Healy nodded. "Okay, Mr. MacAllister, suppose you tell me what this is all about, from the beginning."

The door to the animal shelter flew open, and Cassie emerged.

"That's Cassie Willis," Adam said, "the one who was kidnapped at Lucy Jansen's house."

"Okay, Miss Willis," Healy said as Cassie hurried to Adam's side. "What's going on?"

"Well, uh—" She glanced at Adam. "Hal Tinley and I thought something was wrong at Lucy Jansen's house, so we went to check on her. I looked through a window, and I saw two men in her house. They were yelling at her, and one of them hit her. Hal went inside, and I was really scared. I called Adam"—she touched Adam's arm—"and he said he would call the police. Then one of them came out and saw me."

"You called it in?" the second officer asked Adam.

He checked the man's nametag. "Yes, Officer Packard. Then I hurried over to Silver Dawn, where Lucy Jansen lives."

The officers nodded, and Healy said to Cassie, "What happened when the man saw you outside?"

"He made me go in. Hal was lying on the floor, and Lucy was tied to a chair. One of them had a gun. I—I said the police are on the way. I think that scared them. One of them said to Lucy, 'This ain't over yet.' Then we heard sirens, and they made me go out to their car. One of them drove. The one with the mustache. The other one sat in the back seat behind me, keeping the gun pointed at me."

"And they brought you here?"

"Yes. Adam called my phone, and the man with the gun answered it. He let me talk to Adam, and he said he would meet us at Boscoe's. I knew Boscoe was a very fierce dog here at the shelter. Adam's a volunteer, so he knew all about Boscoe. But the crooks didn't know."

"Okay," said Packard. "So they were willing to swap you for Adam, here?"

"I guess so. But when we got here, we let Boscoe loose, and he scared them back into their car. He likes me—Boscoe, that is. He's fine with women, but not men. Anyhow, the one holding the gun dropped it, and the dog grabbed it in his teeth."

"That's it right there." Adam pointed to the pistol on the ground. "We haven't touched it, but the dog did."

Officer Packard pulled a latex glove from his pocket and put it on. He bent to retrieve the gun. "I'll put this in an evidence bag," he told Healy and headed for their car.

"They left here in the Rolls Royce, but they didn't take the gun?" Healy asked.

"They were scared of Boscoe," Cassie said. "He's really fierce. The man had dropped it, and Boscoc got hold of it and wouldn't give it up. They jumped in their car to get away from him."

Adam nodded. "And they may have caught on to the idea of me calling you while I was inside."

Healy excused himself and went to confer with his superiors by radio. He came back a moment later.

"Sounds like the others could use our help trying to round up those two," he said. "We think we know exactly who they are, since Miss Jansen described them and said they mentioned Ollie Schwam when they were at her house."

"Yeah, I'm pretty sure they're a couple of his henchmen," Packard said.

Cassie inhaled slowly. "So, we can go home?"

"Just let us get your addresses and phone numbers," the officer said. "And we'll need you to make a full statement at the police station. Can you come in this afternoon? Or tomorrow morning at the latest?"

Adam looked at Cassie. Mentally, he ran over both their work schedules.

"Can we come early tomorrow morning?" he asked. "Like maybe seven thirty?"

"Sure, that's fine." Healy produced two business cards with the police station number on them. "Anything else we should know right now?"

"Not really," Adam said, "except they've got our cell phones."

"They took mine when I got in the car with them," Cassie said.

"And mine when they got here." Adam scrunched up his face. "Do you think you can get them back?"

"Maybe. I'll make sure it's in the report." Healy gave them a brief wave. He and his partner headed for their car.

"What now?" Cassie asked as the patrol car drove out.

"I'd better call Doreen right away."

"Who's she?"

"She manages this place. Let's go inside. I'll check Boscoe's cage, too, before we leave. We need to make sure he's secure."

"He's my hero now," Cassie said. "Without him, who knows what would have happened."

"Yeah. He's rough around the edges, but he's not a bad dog."

Adam led the way inside. He called Doreen first and told her about the damage to the gate. Without giving her all the details, he summarized what led to the incident. "We're going to the police station tomorrow morning early to make statements about the whole thing. You should probably report this too. Vandalism, maybe. Anyway, the cops will know what to call it."

When he hung up, he told Cassie, "She's coming over to make sure all the animals are okay. I think she wants to see how bad the damage is. But she did say the insurance would probably cover it."

Cassie gritted her teeth. "I kind of feel like it's my fault."

"No, it's absolutely not. Those two creeps did it. They're criminals. You have no blame in this at all."

She blinked rapidly. "Adam, do you think those guys will come after us again?"

He sucked in a breath. "I hope not."

They held a long gaze, and finally Cassie looked away. "Is it okay if I call Jenna?"

"Sure. I'll go check on Boscoe."

Adam left the lobby, and Cassie picked up the desk phone's receiver.

All of the dogs in the kennels started barking when he entered the canine area. "Settle down, guys," Adam said. He quickly checked Boscoe's cage door and passed out small treats to the inmates.

When he got back to the lobby, Cassie had the phone receiver to her ear.

"Cassie?" Jenna yelled so loudly on the other end that Adam could hear her.

Cassie winced and held the phone several inches away from her cheek. "Yeah, it's me." Her gaze flicked over the phone's base and she pushed a button.

"Where are you?" came Jenna's voice, now on speaker. "I've been trying to call you for the last hour."

"Uh, sorry about that. I'm at the animal shelter." A couple of dogs still barked in the background, as if to confirm her statement.

"What are you doing there?" Jenna demanded.

"It's a long story. I'll tell you when Adam brings me home." Cassie gave him a weak smile. She looked exhausted.

"Well, get here quick," Jenna said. "Your mom's here, and she's worried half sick about you."

Cassie's eyes widened and she met Adam's gaze, shock splashed across her face.

CHAPTER
EIGHTEEN

Adam made sure the shelter was secure, and they headed for his truck. "I guess I should take you straight home," he said.

"Yeah … Jenna or my mom can take me to pick up my car later." Most people probably found it comforting to see their mother right after a harrowing experience, but Cassie was not looking forward to it.

She replayed her mother's voice in her head. Jenna had handed the phone to Mrs. Willis shortly after answering Cassie's call. Cassie had avoided giving details about her day, saying that she had lost her phone and would explain when she got there. *She seemed really freaked out. This is not going to be fun.*

"Do you want me to go in with you?" Adam asked.

His presence had been reassuring ever since the discovery of the body, but thinking of the fresh barrage of questions it would provoke from her mother made Cassie cringe. "Not this time."

"Okay. I think I'm going to get a prepaid phone to use until I find out if the police are likely to recover mine. I can pick one up for you too."

"I'd appreciate that. It's a good idea."

Cassie's mind was whirling with all that had happened in the last hour or two. "Oh! Is Lucy all right? And Hal?"

"They're fine. I asked Kieran not to mention to the cops that I was there …"

"So, those *were* fake sirens?"

"Yeah. Kieran's karaoke machine. I was really hoping they'd just come running out and make a break for it. Honestly, it wasn't much of a plan, but we had to try something." Adam shrugged, looking a little sheepish.

"Hey, it did get them outside. They just took me with them."

"Did they hurt you?"

"Nah. I cooperated. So, why did you tell Kieran not to mention you?"

"I didn't want to be stuck there answering questions, and I knew they wouldn't let me go to the shelter to meet the thugs who took you, so I left in a hurry. I guess the cops will want to question me again at some point, and I'll have to explain leaving the scene of a crime."

"They probably have enough bigger fish to fry that they won't charge you."

"That's what I'm hoping. Man, I can't believe this crazy day. I hope you'll agree with me now that you need to leave well enough alone."

"I'll agree that I've had enough excitement for now, anyway. And I sure don't like being a hostage."

"Hmm."

"But you were really brave to offer to trade places with me, even if you thought Boscoe could get us out of it."

Adam didn't appear flustered at her compliment. He may have been too distracted. "Hey, by the way, I think from the way Boscoe acted over that gun that I might be able to start rehabilitating him. He hated those men, but it seemed like he hated the gun more."

"Yeah, you're right." Cassie remembered Boscoe closing his

jaws around the gun as much as Rumble's hand and the way the dog's attention had been fixed more on the gun than on the men taking shelter in the car.

"If it was an incident with a gun that made him hate men in the first place, if he gets over his fear of guns, maybe he'll stop hating men."

"I hope so. That would be great." Cassie's smile faltered when Adam pulled his truck up in front of her building. "Well … thanks for the ride."

"Of course." Adam reached over to take Cassie's hand. "I'm so glad you're safe now. Maybe I seemed brave, but I was scared. I was praying the whole time."

"Me too." Cassie squeezed his hand. "Get home safe."

In the hall outside her apartment, Cassie took a deep breath and willed herself to be calm before she opened the door. There was her mother, dressed in high-waisted jeans and a button-down blouse. Her light brown hair was pulled back in a messy ponytail.

"Cassie!" Mom rushed forward to hug her. "Where have you been? Jenna told me it's your day off, and you've been gone all day. You weren't answering your phone."

"Like I said, I lost it." Cassie halfheartedly hugged her mom back. "I'm fine. Just a little rattled and frustrated."

"Do you work tomorrow?"

"Yes."

"You want dinner?" Jenna asked. "I made stir fry. It's a little cold."

Cassie gave her a grateful look. "I can heat some up. Thank you. But I should shower first. Mom, you mind?"

Cassie thought she looked like she minded, but she said, "Go ahead."

The shower felt good and helped Cassie calm her nerves,

although she couldn't completely shake off the stress of what was waiting for her when she emerged from the bathroom. She dried off quickly, pulled on some pajamas, and wrapped her hair in a towel before going out to face the music.

Jenna gave Cassie a plate to warm up, along with raised eyebrows that seemed to say, "So sorry you had to live with her your entire childhood."

Cassie knew her mother's line of sight was blocked, so she rolled her eyes in return before taking her plate to the microwave.

"So," her mother prompted. "Where were you all day?"

There was no way Cassie wanted to tell her mother she had been kidnapped. She wasn't sure she could take it, but she didn't want to lie either. "I was a few places. This morning I went to see Ellsborough racetrack with a friend."

"Racetrack? As in horse racing? What made you do a thing like that?"

"One of the older ladies on my pickup route likes to make a bet now and then, and she got me curious about the track."

"Thank goodness she didn't get you curious about tattoos! You'd have been down at the corner tattoo parlor."

"Oh, Mom. I just like horses. It's not like I was gambling."

"That trash business hasn't been good for you. I really think you should find something else."

"The whole point was to keep this job until I find another one. If I find something better, I'll quit."

"Are you actually looking for something better?"

The microwave beeped, and Cassie was relieved for the chance to turn away, if only for a moment. She carried her plate to the table, where Jenna had laid out silverware and a glass of water for her. "I've been kind of busy lately."

"With what?"

"Church, the old folks at Silver Dawn …"

"That's where that body was found!"

Oops. Desperately, Cassie continued, "… my new boyfriend …"

"Boyfriend? You never said you had a boyfriend." The bait had worked, at least for now.

"Well, I don't know if we're really official. It's a new thing. We met at church. Well, we met over the radio through work first, I guess. It's kind of a funny story."

"He's a good guy," Jenna put in.

"So that's why you don't want to leave the job." Mrs. Willis sounded accusing.

Cassie shrugged. "He's part of it. But like I said, we go to the same church."

"He's a Christian, then."

"Yeah. I mean, I haven't heard his testimony yet, but he acts like it. He prays." She smiled a little. "Prays for me."

"And he took you to the *racetrack*?"

Cassie sighed. "I had to talk him into it, actually. But it was fun." *Mostly. Until the creepy men started following us.* "Anyway, then he had to go to work, and I went to spend time with the old folks, and … Later we went to the animal shelter where Adam volunteers. And somewhere along the way, I lost my phone." She was proud of herself for her clever navigation of dangerous truths. She started shoveling food into her mouth with her fork.

"Adam, hmm? I want to meet him."

I want you to not meet him.

Mrs. Willis went on. "Really, though, I'm surprised at the way you've been acting lately. Your father and I taught you kids to take care of yourselves. I'd expect this kind of thing from Nicky, but not you. Meredith certainly wouldn't behave like this. Out all day with a boyfriend, not answering calls, going to a *racetrack* …"

How many times can I mention that I lost my phone before it sinks in? Cassie tried not to let the comments about her siblings get to her. It seemed as if Meredith could do no wrong in her mother's eyes. And poor Nick—he really didn't try to cause trouble. He just lacked a little common sense sometimes.

"Mom, I'm sorry I worried you. I didn't know you were coming. What are you doing here, anyway?"

"I came to check on you. You didn't seem to take my concerns seriously. That whole thing with the body in the dumpster—was it you that found it?"

Oops. There it is again. "Not exactly."

"But you knew about it. Did you see it?" Her mother looked horrified.

"To be honest, I've been trying not to think about that." It was true. Seeing—not to mention touching—the body was the one part of all this that made Cassie's flesh crawl.

Her mother's features softened. "Well, I guess that explains all the distractions."

There was an awkward silence during which Cassie finished her meal. She had been very hungry. She sipped her water and stared at the table. Then she remembered her car. "Oh, uh … Adam dropped me off. I left my car at Silver Dawn. I'll need a ride to get it. Preferably tonight, since I work tomorrow."

"Can't you get tomorrow off? We could spend the day together. A spa day would be a nice distraction."

"This was my day off. This and Sunday. I can't just take another day."

Jenna seemed to be watching them closely, which might mean she knew there was more going on than Cassie was saying. "I can take you to get your car. Mrs. Willis, do you have somewhere to stay tonight?"

"I reserved a hotel room," Mom answered. "Cassie, you could stay there with me tonight."

Cassie shook her head. "I think sticking to my routine is what I need right now."

"Then meet me for lunch. You get a lunch break, don't you? Invite your boyfriend. What's his name again?"

"Adam. Okay. I will."

"Good. Call me … Oh, you don't have your phone."

"That's all right. There's a diner not far from one of my stops. I'll put it in your phone so you can find it. Twelve-thirty should work."

"All right."

Cassie looked up the restaurant on her mother's phone, saved the location, and handed the phone back. "If I don't find my phone soon, I'll get a temporary one. Actually, Adam offered to get me one."

"Hmm. So, he's a gentleman at least."

"At least."

Her mother's eyes brightened as Cassie took her last bite. "Well, why don't I take you to get your car? We can get out of Jenna's way and catch up some more."

Jenna waved a dismissive hand. "You're really not in my way."

"We can catch up at lunch tomorrow," said Cassie. "I'm pretty tired."

Seemingly defeated at last, her mother said, "All right. But you be careful driving. They say driving sleepy is as bad as driving drunk."

"I'll be careful. I promise."

———

Cassie felt immense relief when she shut the passenger door of Jenna's Toyota.

Jenna got into the driver's seat and started the car. "So … did I miss something?"

"Yeah. A lot. I wasn't about to tell my mother I got kidnapped."

Jenna's eyes widened and she stared at Cassie. "Are you serious?"

"Yup. I'll tell you what happened on the way."

By the time they got to the Silver Dawn cul-de-sac, Cassie had told Jenna about the confrontation at Lucy's house, her abduction, and Adam's rescue plan.

"I can't believe this! You're so lucky you're all right. Kidnappings go bad so often. I watch all those true crime things, you know? Cassie …"

"I know. And if my mom knew, she would flip out, big time. She can't find out."

"Got it. Oh, there's your car." Jenna pulled up behind Cassie's gray Ford Focus. "Are your keys in it?"

"No, they're in my purse. I left it at Ed and Flossie's, but their lights are on. I'm glad they're still up."

"I'll wait here until you're back in your car."

"Okay. Thank you."

Grateful for her friend's kindness, Cassie hurried up to Ed and Flossie's door. As she climbed the steps, someone peeked through the curtains of the front window. She knocked.

Almost immediately, Ed answered the door. "Cassie, it's good to see you. We were all so worried."

Flossie's voice came from just behind him. "Come in, dear. I have your purse."

Ed moved aside, and Cassie stepped into the front hall. "I can't stay, but it's good to see you too," she said. "I'm fine, though. My roommate brought me back for my car."

Flossie handed Cassie her purse and patted her hand. "We all agreed, in light of everything that happened, we'll all tell what we know as soon as possible. We'd like to do it all together, but the police have already arranged to meet with some of us because of what happened today, so we're just going to try to give our statements as we're able."

"I see. I'm so sorry about everything you've been through. It isn't fair that this happened in your neighborhood."

"Maybe not fair, but everything happens for a reason," Flossie said.

"That's true. Thank you for keeping an eye on my purse." Cassie took out her keys.

"Of course, dear. Will we see you tomorrow?"

"I'm planning on it."

"See you tomorrow, then," Ed said. "You be careful, Cassie."

"I will."

She slipped her purse strap over her shoulder and walked back to her car, raising her keys to wave at Jenna as she went by.

Jenna rolled down her window. "Hey!"

Cassie walked closer to her friend's car. "What's up?"

"Trav just called me. They arrested those two guys—the ones that kidnapped you—today."

"Really? That's terrific!"

"Yeah, but listen." Jenna leaned out the window and lowered her voice. "You can't say anything to anyone. Travis wasn't supposed to tell me, and I'm not supposed to tell you. But I thought you'd feel better if you knew."

"You got that right." Cassie huffed out a breath. "Wow. I guess I didn't expect them to find them so fast."

"There's one thing, though."

"What?"

"They both claim they know nothing about the dead man in the dumpster. They say they didn't shoot him, and they didn't put him in there."

Cassie frowned. She knew who put Jeff's body in the dumpster. But if Rumble and Mustache didn't kill him, who did?

"Maybe they're lying."

Jenna shrugged. "Maybe. Let's head on home. I'll follow you."

Bright and early, Cassie crept out to the front room. Jenna's phone was fully charged, so she unplugged it and called Reuben's Rubbish Removal. She was surprised when Adam answered.

"Hi, it's Cassie. I wanted to let you know I'm still coming for my truck, even though I don't have a phone."

"Cassie, you should take today off. Archie will understand. I can cover your route, or I can get someone else to take it."

"Aren't you the pot calling the kettle black? You didn't stay home today, and someone pointed a gun at you yesterday."

There was a pause. "Okay, you got me."

"Seriously, I just want some routine right now. I think you understand that."

"Tell you what: I'll give your Meyer Street leg to someone else. That way you can take your time on the rest. And if you want to go home early, just let me know and I'll fix it."

It was a kind offer. "Okay. Thanks, Adam."

"You're welcome."

She hesitated. "Hey, I'm probably not supposed to mention this, but I don't know why not. It should be public knowledge today."

"What?"

"Travis said last night they'd arrested Mustache and Rumble."

"Who?"

"Mustache and Rumble—that's what I call those two guys who kidnapped me. But they say they didn't kill Jeff Patterson."

"Huh."

Cassie rushed on, "And my mother would like you to come with me to have lunch with her today. I can give her an excuse if you'd rather not."

"No, I'd like to meet her."

"All right. But don't say a word about all the hullabaloo."

"Of course not."

She was glad he sounded so confident about meeting her mom. She gave him the name of the diner and prepared to say goodbye.

"Cassie …"

She breathed slowly, not wanting to miss what he said.

"I'm really glad you're all right."

"Yeah. Me too. I'll talk to you later."

"Bye."

She plugged Jenna's phone back in and sighed. She felt strangely warm. Adam made her feel safe, but it was more than that. *Am I in love?*

A couple of hours later, she approached the dumpster at Silver Dawn. Her elderly friends popped out of their homes like the Munchkins after the wicked witch was killed. Even Kieran was there, hanging around conspicuously with a string trimmer —but there didn't seem to be any weeds on that side of the cul-de-sac.

Since Adam had bought her extra time today, Cassie stopped her truck before anyone compelled her to do so. She climbed out of the cab as someone started an impromptu round of applause.

She grinned. "Oh, come on. It's not like I'm a hero or anything."

"We're just happy you're okay," Gerald said.

Lucy stepped forward and grabbed her hand. "You were so brave. Ed told us all last night that you were all right."

"I'm sure glad nothing happened to you," said Kieran.

"We won't keep you from your work." Nita looked around pointedly, and the others nodded and agreed.

"But come back when you can," Hal said.

The group began to disperse.

Cassie turned toward Kieran. "Adam told me you were a big help. Thank you."

Kieran rubbed the back of his neck, blushing a little. "It was the least I could do. I sure didn't mean for you to get mixed up in everything."

She almost laughed. "Why should any of this be your fault?"

He didn't look up, but merely shrugged.

Something felt strange. "Kieran ... do you know something about those men who were at Lucy's?"

"Huh? No. I have no idea who they were."

"Okay. Something else, then?"

Kieran looked downright sick. "I ... I think I made a mistake. I just didn't know what to do."

Cassie's heartbeat suddenly picked up the pace. "Do about what?"

CHAPTER
NINETEEN

Cassie eyed Kieran closely. "What aren't you telling me?"

"Oh, man! I am in so much trouble." Kieran clenched his teeth.

Guilt swept over Cassie. She'd never really liked the young man, but that didn't mean she should have treated him badly. Looking back, it seemed every time Kieran spoke to her she'd responded in a negative way—not just her words, but even her tone.

She reached out and laid her hand on his sleeve. "Kieran, I'm sorry if I've treated you badly. It's true I don't want to go out with you. I don't think we'd be good together. But I still should have been more of a friend to you. If I can help you now, please let me. Tell me what's wrong."

He closed his eyes for a second and pulled in a deep breath. "If I say anything, I'll go to jail."

"What? No! Hey, you helped us yesterday, in a big way."

"But it's all my fault."

"What's your fault?" It hit her suddenly and she jerked upright. "You—you don't mean Jeff Patterson."

Kieran nodded, his face contorted. "I think ..."

"What, Kieran?" Cassie tried to soften her tone, truly

regretting shutting him out so completely. If no one listened to Kieran—really listened to his deepest concerns—what would become of him? He was obviously tortured by something in connection with the crimes that had happened at Silver Dawn. She didn't want to be the person who ignored his pain.

"I think I might have ..." He swallowed hard. "I think I killed him."

She couldn't stop her eyes from flying wide open, but she swallowed the protests of disbelief that sprang to her lips. What sort of person thought he'd killed a man who was obviously dead but didn't know for sure? She shot up a silent prayer for wisdom.

"Okay," she said slowly. "Why do you think that?"

"I saw him Friday morning. The morning before ... before he was in the dumpster."

"You saw him alive that morning?"

Kieran nodded. "I was afraid if I said anything, they'd arrest me."

"But ... where did you see him? And what time?"

"It was over by Gerald's driveway, early. Dad told me I had to weed the flowerbeds by the community center that day, and I wanted to get done as early as I could, so I could go over to the lake in the afternoon and take the boat out. I walked over from our house, and I saw this guy lurking on the sidewalk."

"Jeff Patterson?"

"Yeah. I recognized him when I got close. I'd seen him around here before, but it was awful early to be visiting old people, you know? I said, 'Jeff, what are you doing here?' He turned around, and he had a gun in his hand."

Cassie's pulse tripped, and she made herself pull in a slow breath. "Okay. Then what?"

"He pointed it at me and said, 'Mind your own business, Kieran. You never saw me.' And I ... I felt like he was going to do something bad."

Cassie nodded. She'd think that too. "What did you do?"

"He took a step back and tripped over one of those solar

light things and I thought, now's my chance. I don't normally do things like this, but I thought he'd been watching Miss Lucy's house. I like her, and I didn't want him to do anything bad to her. So I jumped him when he was off balance."

"What did you think he would do?"

"I dunno. Maybe rob her? But then—" He gulped.

Cassie waited for him to go on. When he didn't speak, she said softly, "You said you jumped him."

"Yeah. I hoped I could make him stop whatever it was he planned to do. The gun—it was between us. We kind of wrestled, and I knew I had to get it away from him. We ended up over by Ed and Flossie's when it happened."

Stunned, Cassie stared at his flickering brown eyes.

"I thought he was going to shoot me. Because I bothered him, you know? He was hanging onto the gun and pushing against me. If he got me to back off, I just knew he'd shoot." Kieran looked into her eyes with a helpless plea. "I didn't mean to do it, Cassie, but I thought I was going to die. It just ... went off."

She nodded, thinking about that morning. "But nobody heard the shot. Or did they?"

"I guess it was muffled, kind of. The gun was sort of squished up between us, you know? And it was early. Most of the seniors don't get out and about that early. Sure sounded loud to me, though."

"Didn't anyone come outside?"

"I didn't see anyone. But when Jeff collapsed against me, I didn't know what to do. He fell down on the ground at the Simonsons' walkway. I—I guess I was in shock."

"Where was the gun?" The police hadn't found a gun in the dumpster. Cassie frowned at him. "Tell me, Kieran."

"I panicked. I picked it up and tossed it."

"Where?"

"Kind of across the road, I guess. And I ran."

Cassie considered that. "And you still didn't see anyone?"

He shook his head vigorously. "Nobody."

"But they didn't find the gun when I was here that day."

Kieran crossed his arms over his ribs. "I know. I stayed around our house for a while, wondering what to do. Then my dad asked if I'd weeded the flowerbeds. I hadn't, and he told me to get at it." He swallowed hard and met her gaze. "I was scared. I'd been expecting to hear sirens, and I couldn't figure out why nobody had called the police or anything. It was almost time for you to show up and collect the trash, so I walked over here again. But when I got here—"

"When you got here, what?" Cassie glanced toward the walkway in front of Ed and Flossie's house.

"There didn't seem to be anything wrong. Some of the people were walking around, chatting like everything was normal. And there was nobody lying on the walkway. So then I thought, maybe Jeff wasn't hurt that bad. Maybe he called someone to pick him up."

Cassie found that hard to believe. Jeff had been shot in the chest. But she supposed Kieran hadn't realized at the time that it was a fatal wound.

"So, then what happened?"

"You came. Everyone was watching you get the dumpster, like it was a show or something. I went over to stand with them. I thought maybe I could ask some of them if they'd seen or heard anything odd that morning. And—and then he fell out of the dumpster into your truck." He turned anguished eyes on her. "I couldn't believe it. I didn't want you to get in trouble, but ..."

"You were right to speak up." Cassie exhaled slowly. "Kieran, you have to tell the police."

His Adam's apple jerked. "I figured. But my dad will kill me." He winced, as though realizing what he'd said.

She touched his arm. "I'm sorry. I don't know what will happen, but it sounds like it was accidental. You have to tell them,"

Kieran's whole frame drooped. "There's more."

Cassie eyed him keenly. "How do you mean?"

"Well, I thought it was really odd they didn't find the gun."

"Yes, so do I."

"I didn't dare ask if anyone found one. I know the police didn't, but they weren't looking down near where it happened, by Ed and Flossie's."

"Right."

"I thought about it all weekend. Then Monday night, it rained hard. My dad told me Tuesday morning to clean out the storm drains. A few of them were blocked, and water was running along the sidewalk."

Slowly, Cassie nodded. "I saw you Tuesday morning with a rake."

"Right."

"And?"

"It was in one of the drains all along, right across from the Simonsons'. It was all covered with mud and sticks."

"What did you do?"

Kieran pressed his lips together for a moment then sniffed. "When I realized what it was, I—I pulled it out and stuck it under my sweatshirt."

"What did you do with it?"

"I took it to the toolshed and hid it under a sack of rock salt we use on the walks in the wintertime when it's slippery."

"Oh, Kieran. Is it still there?"

"I think so. But I'm scared that my dad will find it."

She nodded. "Listen, I'm supposed to stay on schedule with my trash run."

"I'm sorry. I shouldn't—"

"No, you should. I'm glad you told me. But I need to get moving. I think you should call someone though. Those men took my phone, so I don't have one—"

Kieran rummaged in his back pocket. "I have mine."

"Great. You can call the police."

His face blanched. "I ... I ..."

175

"Do you want me to call?"

He held out his phone, not meeting her gaze.

Cassie took it but hesitated. If she called 911, she'd get a dispatcher who would follow the impersonal protocol. She considered calling Adam but decided she shouldn't. Instead, she called Jenna and asked for Travis's phone number.

"Cassie! What on earth?"

"Calm down," she told her roommate. "I'm fine, but something's come up concerning the dumpster case. I wanted Travis's opinion."

Jenna huffed out a breath. "Okay, but I'll get the details later, one way or another."

Cassie had no doubt. As soon as Jenna gave her Travis's number, she called him. Kieran stood by, watching her uneasily.

"Trav? It's Cassie." Quickly she outlined what Kieran had told her.

"And he has the gun?"

"He says he hid it, but he thinks it's still there."

"Okay, can you stay with him—"

"I really need to get to work. Mr. Reuben won't like it if—"

"Five minutes, Cassie. I'll be there, and I'll call Detective Mitchell. I just don't want you to leave that guy alone until we get there."

"All right, but hurry." She ended the call and gave Kieran his phone. "I'm sorry, but we had to tell them. The officer I talked to, Travis Doake, is a friend. He's a good guy. He said he has to tell Detective Mitchell, but I think Travis will get here first. Talk to him. He'll be here to help you."

"What if they handcuff me and shove me on the ground and—"

"Well, they might put cuffs on you, I don't know. But they won't hurt you."

"I've seen things on TV."

"I know. Just cooperate with them and do whatever they say. Show them where it happened, and where you found the gun."

He nodded. "If they take me away, will you tell my folks?"

"The police will probably send someone to talk to them. But I'll come by your house tonight, whatever happens." Against her better judgment, she moved in and gave him a quick hug. "You're doing the right thing."

She stepped back. Tears glistened in Kieran's eyes.

In response to her quick call, Adam agreed to meet her a few minutes early for lunch. As soon as Travis arrived, Cassie left him with Kieran and quickly collected Silver Dawn's trash. As she drove the truck out of the senior complex, she saw Detective Mitchell pull his unmarked car in behind Travis's cruiser.

Though she hurried through her next few pickups, she still had to drive the garbage truck to the diner. There wasn't time to go to RRR and retrieve her car. She parked at the far end of the lot and hurried toward the little restaurant. Adam waited just outside the door, staring at her truck.

"Do you think Mom will notice that I arrived here in a garbage truck?"

"Uh, probably. And she's due here any minute."

Cassie shook her head. "Sorry I'm later than anticipated. A lot has happened." Rather than tell her tale inside the small diner with other customers nearby, she pulled him to one side and swiftly unfolded Kieran's tale of woe.

"Wow. He really didn't think the guy was dead?" Adam asked.

"Well, I think he did, but when the body disappeared ..."

"Okay, I get it. But the police are there now?"

"Yeah, Travis came right away, and Detective Mitchell arrived as I was leaving."

Adam nodded and held out a plastic store bag. "Well, I got our new phones. Yours is in here. I already set it up and put my new number in it for you."

"Thank you so much." Cassie peeked inside the bag.

"Your new number's on the paper in there. I thought it was best to get new numbers, in light of who has our old phones now."

"Probably a good idea, although if the police recovered them we may get them back."

"Oh, is that your mom?"

Cassie followed his gaze and spotted her mother's red Tesla rolling toward an open parking space. "That's her. Mum's the word."

"Right."

"Best behavior."

"I can't wait to meet her."

Cassie grabbed his hand and pulled him toward the Tesla as her mother emerged.

"Mom! This is Adam."

Adam grinned and extended his hand. "I'm so happy to meet you, Mrs. Willis."

Her mother seemed mildly surprised that they weren't waiting for her inside at a table, but Cassie chattered brightly and hurried her to the entrance, hoping she wouldn't spot the trash truck.

"Dear, you came in jeans?" Mom eyed her outfit critically.

"Well, I came right from work."

"It's very informal here," Adam said quickly, pulling the door open and standing to one side.

They were soon seated and placing their orders. Mom seemed to accept Adam's recommendation of a club sandwich after he assured her the diner's staff did a great job.

"It's very casual." Mom looked around after the waitress had left them.

"Yes, a lot of people pop in here for lunch on workdays," Cassie said.

"Well, Adam MacAllister, tell me about yourself." Her mother sat back and seemed to relax a little, smiling at Adam.

He stepped up, keeping the cheerful conversation flowing throughout their meal, and Cassie learned a few new things about Adam herself. She hadn't known before that he had lost his father at ten, or that his mother was remarried. She had a distinct feeling her mother liked him, especially when he insisted on paying for their lunch.

They rose and headed toward the door.

"So, how long will you be in Knottsville, Mrs. Willis?" Adam asked as he held the door for them.

"I'm not sure yet. I just came to check on Cassie, but she seems to be doing all right. I hoped we could spend some leisure time together."

"Not on weekdays, Mom." Cassie tried to keep her impatience out of her voice. "I told you, I don't have a lot of free time until Saturday."

"Oh, well, we'll see." Mom looked around. "Where's your car, dear?"

Cassie gulped.

Adam said quickly, "Her car's back at the office. I'll take her back there to get it."

"Oh. All right."

Her mother gave Cassie a kiss on the cheek. "I'll see you this evening, honey."

"Right. You'll have supper with me and Jenna?"

"I'd love to. We can talk more then." She turned to Adam. "I'm so glad we got to meet today, Adam."

"Me too, Mrs. Willis. I'm sure we'll see each other again before you leave town."

"Good. I'd like that."

Mom strode toward her car, and Adam guided Cassie toward his.

"Just make it look like we're leaving together," he said softly. "I don't think she even noticed the Triple-R truck."

"Let's hope not." Cassie waved as her mother pulled out

onto the street, then she turned to face him. "Okay, I've got my afternoon route to do, and I'd better get to it."

"Right. I'll get back to the office." Adam hesitated then leaned forward and brushed her lips with his. "I'll call you tonight."

Cassie smiled as she turned away. She pulled up short as a man approached them. He was only about five yards away, and there was no mistaking him. Mr. Mustache. She froze, her heart sinking.

"Miss Willis."

She gulped. "A-Adam?"

He hurried to her side, glowering at the kidnapper. "What do you want?"

"Just a quick word with Miss Willis."

"You leave her alone." Adam stepped forward, his fists clenched.

Cassie reached for his arm. No way did she want another dust-up with Mr. Mustache.

"I thought you were in jail," she blurted.

Mustache narrowed his cold, dark eyes. "I was. They let me go."

"How come?" Adam said. "You kidnapped her."

"Let's just say I had a get-out-of-jail-free card."

Fury boiled up in Cassie. "Oh yeah? What about your friend Rumble? Is he walking loose too?"

Mustache blinked at her then cracked a smile. "Rumble. That's pretty good. His name's Clarkson. And no, he's still in custody."

She swallowed hard. "Why are you following us—again?"

Adam put his hand on her shoulder, eyes on Mustache.

Mustache's expression was blank. "I just want to tell Miss Willis to be careful."

Cassie's scowl deepened. "Is that a threat?"

"It's just a warning. I don't mean you any harm."

"You made me go into Lucy's house at gunpoint."

"And you unleashed a vicious dog on me."

"Fair enough." She clamped her lips together.

Mustache looked at Adam. "Just keep your heads down. Both of you, but especially Miss Willis. She's made an enemy."

"Meaning you?" Cassie snapped.

"No. Not me." Mustache turned and hurried away, slipping quickly between the parked vehicles.

She turned to Adam. "What was that?"

"I don't know, but whether he was being honest or not, there's no harm in being careful."

"That's true."

"Let's do as he says and get out of here. I'll walk you to your truck."

CHAPTER
TWENTY

Adam did his best not to show how much Mustache's appearance had rattled him. His heart drummed from unused adrenaline as he stood beside Cassie's truck, holding her open door. "I think I'm going to call Detective Mitchell. He should know about this."

"Okay." Cassie still looked shaken too.

"I'll give you a call after I talk to him. And I want you to report in after each pickup you do. Either text me or use the radio. I know it's a pain, but I want to make sure you're safe."

She gave him a wan smile. "Okay."

He squeezed her hand, then stepped back to close her door. He watched her back the truck around and returned her wave before heading for his pickup. He didn't have Mitchell's number in his new phone, but he could look up the police station's number back at the office and ask for him.

About twenty minutes later he had Mitchell on the phone.

"What can I do for you, Mr. MacAllister?"

"Well, I'm not sure." Adam explained what had happened at the diner, giving the detective as much detail as he could remember. He waited on hold for a couple of minutes before Mitchell returned.

"All right. I won't tell you not to worry about it, but I think you can be reasonably sure that Stevens isn't out to get you himself."

At least we can stop calling him Mr. Mustache. "How come he's not in custody anymore?"

"I can't say specifically. He's involved in an open case."

"Should I take Cassie off the work roster for now? Is she in danger on her route?" Adam hoped he was overreacting.

"Probably no more than she is at home. I'm going to arrange for an unmarked car to drive by her apartment every hour or so in the evening, to make sure everything is quiet. If she sees anything suspicious, she can call me, or of course 911 if she feels like she's in danger. Like I said, I can't be specific but try not to worry. I think we should be able to update you soon."

Adam didn't like the thought that Cassie could be in danger at home, but he was grateful that the detective was taking his concern seriously enough to have someone check on her. "All right. Thank you. I'll tell her what you said."

After he took a minute to make sure all his other drivers were on schedule, Adam called Cassie.

"Hello," she said over some heavy white noise. "Sorry it's loud. I'm driving, so I put you on speaker."

"That's okay. I got ahold of Detective Mitchell. Mr. Mustache's name is Stevens." He went on to tell her about the drive-by checks.

"I don't know if I'm relieved or unnerved that they're taking that step," Cassie said. The loud creak of her truck's brakes interrupted them for a moment.

"I know, but I'm trying to see it as a good thing. He got kind of cryptic on why Stevens wasn't detained. Something about him being involved in an open case, so he couldn't tell me."

"That's weird. I wonder if Travis would know why."

"Cassie, I think it's best if we don't snoop anymore."

"Hey, Kieran came to me about what happened with him and Jeff. I didn't go looking for that information."

"I know. Anyway, Mitchell said he thought they could give us an update soon. Can we at least let it lie until then?"

"I'm not going to *do* anything. I'm just curious."

Adam hmphed. He was getting used to the concept that Cassie didn't know how to leave well enough alone. "I don't like the sound of that."

"If I come to any major conclusions, I'll let you know."

"Fine. I'm going to text Mitchell's number to you so you can contact him if you notice anything weird."

Cassie thanked him. "I'm about to load a dumpster now. I guess I'll let you go, unless there's anything else you need to tell me."

"Nope. We're good. Just be careful."

"I will."

Cassie knew that caution was rarely a bad idea, but she would rather put the encounter with Mr. Mustache out of her mind completely. Things had been stressful enough since yesterday. She prayed, tried a breathing exercise, and even sang to herself to pass the time until Adam called her with the information from Detective Mitchell.

She was glad he had taken the last leg off her route. It meant she could get done a little early and have some free time with Jenna before her mother showed up for dinner. She swung by Silver Dawn as she had promised Kieran, but it looked like no one was home at the Harmons'.

"Do you think your mom will mind if Travis comes over?" Jenna asked as soon as she got home.

Cassie smirked. "No. In fact, I think she'd like to meet him. She has a high opinion of police officers in general."

"Cool. I'll text him."

"Just make sure he knows what he's in for."

"It'll be fine."

After sending her text, Jenna put the chicken parmesan into the oven and Cassie prepped garlic toast while she filled her roommate in on Kieran's confession.

"I can't believe it was that dude who's been hitting on you, and he was there the whole time! Right in plain sight."

"Tell me about it. I feel bad. I pretty much ignored him all I could. I wonder if I would have realized he knew something much sooner if I'd been paying attention."

Jenna sighed. "Well, it's too late now. Don't beat yourself up over it."

They had just started preparing the salad when Cassie's mother arrived.

Mom seemed to be in a decent mood. "Something smells good."

"The chicken is getting hot," Jenna told her. "You should smell our cheater garlic bread soon too."

"Cassie loves her shortcuts."

Cassie mentally shrugged off the comment, even though she suspected her mother was probably thinking about some of her life choices that were more consequential than putting butter and garlic powder on split-top wheat bread. "Jenna's boyfriend, Travis, is coming too. He's a police officer."

"Really? How exciting."

Jenna grinned. "Well, usually the job is kind of boring for him—for which I'm grateful. Traffic tickets, paperwork, the occasional accident response, more paperwork. Much as I'd like him to have some adventures, he's safer when it's quiet."

"Oh, I'm sure. I don't blame you a bit."

Travis announced his arrival with a knock, and Jenna introduced him as they began setting the table.

Cassie wished Travis had arrived earlier, so she could ask him about "Mustache" Stevens without her mother there. She would have to either find a sneaky way to ask him or wait for a better opportunity.

They sat down to eat, and Travis asked the blessing.

Mom sniffed the steam coming off her serving of chicken and smiled. "So, Travis, do you know Cassie's boyfriend?"

"Yeah. We all go to the same church." Travis helped himself to a slice of toast. "We're not buddies or anything, but I guess since Cassie and Jenna are good friends, we might end up hanging out. Adam seems like a good guy."

"I see. I appreciate friends looking out for Cassie. She's had quite a time lately."

Cassie kept her focus on her plate to avoid rolling her eyes. "Hey, um … Travis, didn't someone in your department arrest a couple of guys yesterday?"

Travis was pretty quick on the uptake. He would know she wanted to avoid alerting her mother to her involvement. "Last night, yeah. I wasn't there, though."

"Was it a big arrest? Will they go to jail for a long time?"

"That depends on a few things, but I think it was a pretty serious charge."

"What kind of charge?" Mom asked.

"Armed kidnapping," he answered.

"Oh, no. Is the victim all right?"

Travis's mouth twitched like he wanted to smile but fought it off. "Yes, fortunately. It turned out all right this time."

Cassie decided to take a shot at more information. "When someone gets arrested for something like that, they don't usually get released right away, right?"

"No. They'd at least have to wait until bail is set, and for a felony, the bail will be high."

"How long would that take?"

"In this case, the earliest they could post bail would be the next morning. It could take a day or two though."

Cassie took a bite of chicken, avoiding looking at her mother.

Mom seemed not to suspect anything so far. "Imagine

someone dangerous like that getting out on bail the next day! Is this a dangerous neighborhood?" She sounded worried.

"I don't think so," said Travis. "Knottsville is usually pretty quiet. We get more activity closer to downtown Ellsborough."

Jenna spoke up. "Where Cassie and I rarely go, even during the day."

"Glad to hear it." Mom helped herself to a generous serving of salad.

Cassie tried once more. "If a kidnapper or murderer or someone like that did get released right away, what might be the reason?"

That might have been going too far. Mom looked sharply at her. "Cassie, what are you going on about? Is there some dangerous criminal out walking around Knottsville?"

Cassie shrugged, trying to look nonchalant. "I'm curious about procedure."

"There could be a few reasons for that," said Travis. "For instance, they might want the crook free so they can tail him to a bigger crook. Or he could be a confidential informant or even an undercover cop. Or it could just be a matter of not having strong enough evidence and wanting to wait until we're sure the charges will stick. But when we arrest someone for kidnapping, we generally have all the evidence we need."

"Right."

Cassie abandoned the topic after that and let the others direct the conversation. While Travis helped Jenna with the dishes, she let her mother catch her up on news from back home. Then she mentioned that she had to get up early again the next day, and her mom took the hint. After a little more chatting, she said she should be leaving.

Cassie walked to the door with her. "If you're staying in town, maybe tomorrow night Adam and I can pick you up for prayer meeting."

"Sure, I'd like that." Mom hugged her. "Have a good night, dear."

Once the door closed behind her mother, Cassie looked at Travis. She'd been thinking hard about what he'd said earlier. "Since you're off duty, can I ask you some more questions? Just out of curiosity, of course."

Travis snorted. "Okay, but make it quick. I need to get going too."

"How might a person tell if someone is a confidential informant or an undercover cop? Or for that matter, if they've been turned loose so the cops can follow them?"

Jenna glanced between them, eyes wide with interest.

"If they're good, you can't tell." Travis looked thoughtful. "I guess if they've been released and aren't sure why, they'll either be overconfident or very nervous. You know, proud of getting away, or worried his cronies will think he's a CI or a cop. If he's a CI, he's in it for himself. All he cares about is money and his own skin. He's not trained like a cop, so if he's not a habitual liar, he might act nervous. But he also won't have to get rid of the cop habits—standing a certain way, keeping your back to the wall, wearing certain clothes. It takes a lot of practice to unlearn certain things and blend in."

"That makes sense." Cassie tried to remember Stevens's demeanor. Had he been overconfident? Nervous? Lying for some sordid reason? If he was really warning them for their own good, did that rule out the CI possibility?

She excused herself to let Jenna say goodbye to her boyfriend privately. While she brushed her teeth and got ready for bed, she pictured Stevens and recalled the way he spoke that day. *I just don't know enough to be sure.* She sighed, knowing she would probably have to wait for that update from Detective Mitchell.

Predictably, when she returned to the front room, Jenna pounced.

"What happened today that I don't know about? Spill."

It's just another day at work. Cassie got into her garbage truck Wednesday morning after stopping at the office briefly to have a cup of coffee with Adam. She mentioned Travis's ideas about Stevens, but Adam seemed to have his mind on other things. She figured she would get a lecture about minding her own business if she kept talking about it, so she brought up taking her mother to prayer meeting instead. Adam had agreed readily.

She put the truck in gear and hit the road on her Wednesday route, a boring one to her, but that was probably what she needed. No Silver Dawn residents to distract her or add to her stress with their gossip. She should check on them soon, though. Maybe she would go by on her break to see how the police interviews were going. Now that Kieran had come clean, she was sure her friends' innocence was much more plausible to the police.

Cassie glanced in her mirror as she pulled out into traffic after her third stop. She noticed a sleek black sedan leaving the curb several car lengths behind her. *Don't jump to conclusions.*

But it seemed as if she had seen a similar car near her previous stop too. "It's black," she muttered. "Tons of cars are black. People like black cars."

She took a turn earlier than she normally did, and the black car passed by behind her. "Yup, I'm paranoid."

Stevens's warning had gotten into her head. Maybe that was all it was meant to do. Maybe that was his revenge for her siccing a dog on him. She wondered if he or Rumble had to have stitches after Boscoe attacked them.

At lunchtime, she checked on the Silver Dawn residents as planned. Nita was away at her bead shop, and Hal had taken Lucy to the police station to give statements. Gerald, Ed, and Flossie were home. Ed complained that he still didn't have his gun back, even though the cops *knew* it had nothing to do with Jeff's death.

Cassie tried to console him. "I'm sure you'll get it back eventually."

"Maybe in a year or two." Ed shook his head.

Flossie patted his arm. "Oh, I'm sure it won't be that long. I'm just glad they're talking about letting us pay our debt to society through community service. I was afraid we were all going to the hoosegow."

"Is there any news about Kieran?"

"They let him go, at least for now," Ed said. "His father's keeping him on a short leash, though. And the word is, he could still be charged."

"With murder?"

"Well, maybe," Ed said. "More likely manslaughter, I think."

Flossie chimed in. "Somebody said they could charge him with obstructing justice for hiding that gun."

Cassie still felt apprehensive for Kieran, but she left the neighborhood feeling reassured overall. The older residents were all making their statements now, giving the police whatever information they could. She sent up a prayer of thanks for that. The day finally felt normal.

It wasn't until she was leaving RRR in her own car that she saw another new-looking black sedan following her from a distance—or the same one she'd seen earlier.

Her heart thudded too fast for such an insignificant thing, but she couldn't tamp down the anxiety. As she made her way through the outskirts of Ellsborough, other cars got between them. She tried to relax.

Then she turned onto the route that connected the city to her side of Knottsville. The traffic went on while the black car turned onto her road.

It's fine. They're just going the same way.

Cassie hurried a little, letting her speed climb up to five miles per hour over the limit. The black car seemed to maintain its distance behind her, not catching up or falling behind. She eased her foot off the gas pedal, wondering if the black car would pass her.

Again, the car kept its distance, as if the driver wanted exactly five car lengths between them.

Cassie pulled in a shaky breath. *That settles it. They really are following me. And I'm on the loneliest stretch of road between work and home.*

CHAPTER
TWENTY-ONE

Adam kept busy, trying not to think about Cassie or the gangsters they'd inadvertently connected with. One of his drivers had a flat tire, so he had to call out a service truck. When that was finally resolved, he looked up to find Detective Mitchell entering the RRR office.

"Hey. I didn't expect you to come by in person." Would his boss be upset if he came out of his private office to find the police here—again?

"I was in the neighborhood," Mitchell said. "Thought it might be more assuring for you and Miss Willis if you heard it directly from me."

Adam eyed him keenly. "What's that?"

"Well, as I told you, we've got Clarkson in custody, and I don't think he'll be leaving us for a good long while."

"What about the other man—Stevens?"

Mitchell sighed. "I don't think you have to worry about him."

A call came over the radio from the driver who'd had the flat.

"Excuse me," Adam said. "Yeah, seventeen? What's up?"

"Tire's fixed, Mac. I'm heading out."

"Great. Thanks." Adam replaced the radio handset.

"Mac?" Mitchell asked.

"Short for MacAllister." Adam ran a hand through his hair. "Look, I know what you said, but that Stevens guy is—well, frankly, he's a little scary. He followed us around at the racetrack Monday, and then yesterday he popped up at the diner where we had lunch. You say he's not dangerous, but I need a little more convincing."

Mitchell gritted his teeth. "Look, I didn't say he's not dangerous. It's just—" He huffed out an exasperated sigh. "I'm pretty sure he wouldn't hurt you or Miss Willis."

"And what makes you so sure?"

Adam held his gaze until Mitchell looked away.

"I'm not at liberty to say."

"Oh, right." Adam shook his head.

"Believe me, if I could tell you I would."

"Sure you would." Adam glanced toward Mr. Reuben's closed office door. "Why should I trust you? Just because you're a cop?"

Mitchell swallowed. "I know that's not enough nowadays. But I really—" At a sharp ring, he pulled a phone from his pocket and looked at the screen then gave Adam an apologetic look. "Sorry. I have to take this."

Adam waved him away, and Mitchell turned toward the door.

"Yeah?" He stopped walking and listened for a moment, his back rigid. "When? Where is she?" He whirled and locked his gaze on Adam. "Okay, I'll head out there. Keep me posted."

It probably had nothing to do with him and Cassie, but the look on Mitchell's face set Adam's pulse throbbing. Mitchell stepped back toward his desk.

"I'm sorry. It's—it's Miss Willis."

Adam's chest felt as if an anvil had settled on it. "What about her?"

"She called 911. That is, her phone did. But now she's not responding to the dispatcher."

"She ..." Adam jerked around to look at the wall clock. "She was on her way home. She should be getting there within the next ten minutes."

"They're tracking her phone," Mitchell said. "I'm going out there."

"Take me with you."

"I can't." Mitchell strode out the door.

Adam pulled a breath into his constricting lungs. He closed his mouth and tried to swallow down the boulder in his throat. He ran to Mr. Reuben's door and opened it without knocking. "Boss, I need to leave. It's an emergency—Cassie needs me."

Blinking, Archie Reuben stood. "All right, Mac. I'll cover the calls for you."

Adam didn't wait any longer but ran for his truck.

Cassie clung to the steering wheel. Her phone had fallen to the floor as she fumbled to hit 911 while going fifty miles an hour. She couldn't see it now, and when she shuffled her foot around, she couldn't feel it. Did the call go through? If she yelled, would someone hear her?

The car behind her swung into the other lane. No traffic came toward her, and the shiny black car pulled up, closing the gap between them. She could see it in her sideview mirror now. The sun glinting off its windshield kept her from trying to identify the driver.

Lord, help me! What do I do?

The car slid into her blind spot. She threw a quick glance over her shoulder, just long enough to see the black hood inching up on her Focus. Her heart was already pounding, and her breath came in short gasps.

Show me what to do!

She hit the brake hard. If the black car got ahead of her, she'd have more control. Wouldn't she?

It came even with her, and she saw a man at the wheel—not one she recognized. The back seat's windows were tinted, and she couldn't tell if anyone rode behind the driver. She put all her weight on the brake pedal, and for a moment the other car was still gaining. But then its driver must have braked, too, because it no longer moved ahead. Instead, it drifted over the center line toward her.

She looked forward. If she could just make it another half mile, she'd be in a more populated area. Only five or six miles of pavement separated her from home, but right now it seemed like a remote and unreachable target.

Could she make it to the Knottsville police station? She clenched her teeth. The municipal buildings were farther away than her apartment. Jenna would be getting home about now, but if she went home would she endanger Jenna too?

Her frantic calculations ended abruptly as the black car's front quarter panel bumped her fender. Cassie jumped. It wasn't a hard impact, but it was enough to drive her Focus at least a foot toward the side of the road.

She tried to straighten her wheels, but the black car was taking over her space. She swerved to the right and felt her front wheel drop an inch or two off the edge of the pavement.

Breathing seemed impossible. She pumped the brake pedal, hoping she could drop back farther behind her assailant. He braked, too, and the Focus slammed into his rear bumper.

Her car came to a halt at last. The black vehicle didn't speed off as she'd hoped. Instead, she stared at the shattered taillight before her and the unfamiliar logo in the middle of the trunk. A stylized *L* in a circle. Lexus, maybe?

Breathe, she told herself. She felt sick. Before she could think of anything else, she heard a door shut. Was the driver coming back here? Somehow, she doubted he'd calmly ask for her insurance information. She swung her legs up and over the gearshift console. Fumbling for the passenger door handle, she darted a glance to the driver's window. The unknown man approached her car with heavy, deliberate steps. She yanked on the door handle, pushed open the passenger door, and then hit the lock button.

As she jumped out, she realized the road's verge was only a few inches wide, and then it sloped downward a couple of feet. She stumbled. *Whump!* She'd splatted in the narrow gravel strip beside the car. She lay stunned for a moment. Her view beneath her car's undercarriage revealed the man's shoes, expensive-looking brown leather.

Run!

She scrambled to her knees, noting a stabbing pain in her right ankle. She had to run. Why was there no traffic here today? It was almost rush hour.

"Don't move."

She froze, not daring to rise enough to look through the windows. Instead, she hunkered down and looked under the car again. Now there were two sets of shoes. Two men stood beyond her Focus.

"If you run, I will shoot you."

Cassie gasped.

"Come on out, nice and easy."

Snail-like, she edged upward until her eyes topped the bottom edge of her car's passenger window. Two men stood on the other side—the driver and another man whose picture she'd studied online. Ollie Schwam. Both of them held handguns.

Her breath caught. She took a fleeting glance over her shoulder. If she ran down into the ditch, she'd be an easier target. No trees or buildings offered sanctuary. But was her car really a good shield? All they had to do was walk around the trunk, and she'd be fully exposed. She wavered. Maybe it would be best to just surrender.

But, no. She wouldn't let them take her again. She kept crouching in place, clinging to the door handle to steady her.

Another vehicle came toward them—finally—from the direction she'd been heading. Its driver approached the scene slowly and rolled down a window, eyeing the two touching cars. Schwam kept his back to the newcomer, holding his gun close to his body, within the open front of his jacket. His companion shoved his into his waistband.

"Everything okay?" the driver in the brown Jeep called.

"Yeah, we've got it sorted," Schwam's driver replied. "Cops are on the way. Just a fender bender."

The Jeep's driver waved and moved on. Cassie wanted to scream, but the blockade in her throat nearly strangled her. Only a muted squeak came out.

The man in the Jeep was gone, not having noticed her at all.

Schwam's companion pulled out his gun again and started cautiously along the side of her Focus.

"What do you want?" she managed to croak out.

She didn't think they could hear her, but Schwam lifted his chin, looking down his nose at her through the two windows and the interior of her car.

"You really don't know? I'll tell you. You're a problem, Miss Willis. You've been meddling in my business."

"I—no. I haven't, honest."

"You brought the cops down on my people," Schwam said. "Not only that, you interfered with the marks one of my runners was dealing with."

Marks? Does he mean the folks at Silver Dawn? Cassie gulped. A gangster was blaming her for getting in his way?

The driver reached the trunk and headed on around the back of her car. She didn't have a good view of him, but she had the impression of a lanky form, and he was younger than the men who'd kidnapped her, maybe as young as Jeff Patterson. Now he was directly behind her car, and she could see him through the rear window. He might be good-looking if it weren't for that scowl and the pistol in his hand. Her swallow pained her throat.

"Stand up," Schwam barked.

With a jerk, she whipped her attention back to the leader.

His face was set in a cruel sneer. She tried to straighten, but something held her back.

Another car was coming, this time from the way they'd come. She stared at the beat-up Monte Carlo as it pulled up behind her Ford and Schwam's driver stepped out of the way. Someone she did know climbed out of the dark blue sedan.

Mustache! Or Stevens, rather. He had to be following her constantly. She almost wished he'd shown up sooner, before Ollie Schwam and his chauffeur had run her off the road. Why was his boss trailing her now, instead of leaving her in the hands of his henchmen?

"Heard they let you go," Schwam told the newcomer.

"For now, anyway." Stevens walked grimly forward. "What've you got?"

"The meddling girl's back there." Schwam nodded in Cassie's direction, past her car.

"Hiding from you?"

"Not for long," Schwam's driver said.

Stevens took a step, blocking the man from walking between the front of his car and the back of Cassie's. She squinted at them. Was he intentionally holding the driver back?

"I've had enough of her," Schwam said. "What brings you here, Stevens?"

"I heard on the scanner the cops are out looking for her. She dropped off their radar or something?"

Schwam's eyes narrowed. "You think her car's got a tracker?"

"Pinging her phone, I think."

Cassie's head swam. So her call had gone through after all? At least it was on and could lead the police to her. How long did she need to stall this time? She recalled the things Travis had told her about confidential informers. If Stevens was one of those, would he help these two snatch her again? Or would he signal the police as to her location?

Schwam's driver snarled, "Let's get her."

Cassie's heart sped. She had nowhere to hide.

"Easy, now," Stevens said. "We don't want to have any shooting. Besides, the safest place to hide in a gunfight like this is behind a tire."

Cassie's mind boggled at that. Was he telling her where to stay? But CI's only cared about themselves, right?

Schwam snapped, "What are you talking about?"

"There's three of us," the driver protested. "We can get her easy.

"Fine. You go around the front. I'll take the back."

After a moment, the chauffeur said, "I'll have to go clear around the Lexus."

"Do it then," Stevens said.

"What are you up to?" Schwam scowled at Stevens.

"What do you mean?"

"You don't want us to get her. No wonder the cops let you go. You're on their side, aren't you?"

Stevens whipped out his pistol as Schwam swung his handgun toward him. A shot roared, then another.

Cassie scrunched low behind her car's front tire, her heart racing. She'd half expected Schwam to take part in cornering her, along with his two flunkies. But now it sounded as though he didn't trust Stevens anymore. She didn't dare look to see if either of them was wounded. She glanced toward Schawm's car. Where was the driver?

Then she heard him almost blubbering. "Hey, now, take it easy. I-I-I didn't do anything to her. It was Ollie. He wanted to get her."

"Just put your gun down, Pete," Stevens said evenly. "Lay it on the ground. That's it."

A siren yowled in the distance.

"You hear that, Miss Willis?" Stevens called. "It's going to be okay. Just stay where you are until the cops get here."

She gulped in a breath. Was he really trying to help her?

"We gotta go," the driver said, his voice rising. "Help me get Ollie in the car."

"Leave him right there," Stevens said. "The ambulance will get him. And you're not going anywhere."

She heard hurried footsteps.

"Stop," Stevens barked. "If you don't want a hole in you like Schwam, you just stop right there, Pete."

"Please, please—I don't—"

The rest of the driver's frantic plea was drowned out by the wailing siren. At last, Cassie rose to where she could see through the windows. A police car pulled up and parked on the edge of the road just ahead of Schwam's vehicle. Two officers jumped out, their guns drawn, and ran toward the others.

"I'm putting my weapon down," Stevens yelled, and he bent to place his gun on the pavement. "Mr. Schwam is wounded and needs an ambulance. That man is his driver, Pete Nelson. I'm Special Agent Philip Stevens."

Cassie's jaw dropped. Special agent? Wasn't that an FBI designation?

Another police car arrived, and Detective Mitchell got out.

"Stevens! Where's Miss Willis?"

"Behind her car." Stevens nodded in Cassie's direction, and she straightened to her full height and walked carefully along the side of the car toward the trunk.

"Miss Willis! Are you all right?" Mitchell called.

"Y-yes."

A familiar pickup arrived and parked behind Stevens's. Adam jumped out and ran toward her.

CHAPTER
TWENTY-TWO

C assie hurriedly ran a brush through her hair and swiped some foundation over her skin before grabbing her jacket and heading for the door. On the understanding that they would follow up with more details later, the police had agreed to let her and Adam leave the scene of the shooting that afternoon after giving brief statements. They would just have time to pick up her mother before prayer meeting.

"We'd better take my car." She held out her keys to Adam. "You want to drive?"

"Sure. Are you sure you still want to go?"

"We have to go. Otherwise, I would have to explain all this to her."

She hadn't even taken the time to fully explain the situation to Jenna as she breezed through their apartment. Now she and Adam were on their way, a bit harried, but they'd be on time—just barely. She wondered if she could return her breathing to normal by the time they picked up her mother. Adam had decided to save time by not going home to change. His work khakis were nice enough for a Wednesday night.

"I still can't believe Stevens is an FBI agent," Adam said after a tense silence.

"I know. I thought he might be an undercover cop, especially when he told me where to take cover, but FBI! I really want to know more about that." Cassie clutched her Bible case. The adrenaline hadn't completely faded yet.

Adam shook his head with a faint smile. "You always want to know more."

"I can't help it. I have an inquiring mind."

"Mm-hmm."

"Remember, Mom can't know someone ran me off the road. None of it."

"Yes, ma'am. Good thing your car didn't get badly dented up."

"I'll say." She hopped out as soon as he parked at the hotel, thankful the dented fender was on the other side.

Her mother came out to the curb to meet them. She wore a simple black skirt with a flowered blue top that Cassie had seen her wear a few times before.

"Want to sit up front?"

"Oh, no, I'm fine in back," Mom said, and Cassie opened the door for her.

"Sorry we're cutting it so close," Adam told her.

Mom climbed into the back seat, and Cassie closed the door. "Oh, that's all right. These things happen. How was work today?"

Cassie licked her lips. "Uh, kind of stressful, but all's well that ends well. Adam helped me relax a little, and I'm sure church will help too."

"I think things will be calmer for a while after today," Adam said.

"Well, that's good." Mom paused and then gave a little sigh.

"You know I've been worried about you, Cassie, but I can see you're in good company here. I think I'm going to head home tomorrow."

Cassie was glad her mother couldn't see her face from behind her. "Oh? Right away?"

"Well, I think I may have overreacted a bit to the body in the dumpster situation … The whole thing is a horrible business, but it's over, and it's not like you were really in much danger yourself. I'm sorry. I just don't want anything to happen to you."

Cassie stole a glance at Adam. He looked like he was fighting a grin.

"It's fine," she said. "It was kind of shocking, but I heard it was an accidental death and the police are winding down their investigation."

"That's good. Your father wants me to come home, so I guess I will."

To Cassie's relief, her mother let the subject of her job drop. Instead she asked Adam about his education and what kind of church he grew up in. That was all she had time for before they arrived.

As they entered the sanctuary, Cassie remembered she had agreed to play the piano that evening. She hurriedly informed her mother and gave Adam's hand a squeeze to apologize for leaving him to fend for himself. She walked briskly to the piano and slid onto the bench, opening the hymnal to a familiar chorus. As she began to play, the chatter died down, and when she finished the final bars, Pastor Nickerson took his place at the pulpit.

She accompanied two hymns, played an offertory that was largely improvised since she had forgotten to practice, then accompanied more singing before the sermon. By the time she got to the seat her mother and Adam had kept for her between them, she had calmed.

The service helped to clear her mind. She knew God was in control, that He had orchestrated everything for His purpose— from her finding the body nearly two weeks earlier, to meeting Adam at church, to Stevens showing up in time to protect her. She felt at peace now.

She looked up at Adam as they walked out of the church together. He was the one thing she wasn't settled about. The last few times they had seen each other, it had been in the midst of a harrowing experience. She liked him a lot, but was the adventure clouding her judgment?

To look at him, no one would know how upset Adam had been earlier when he rushed to her side by the road. She had been shaking with fear, but once he embraced her, she felt completely safe. He'd asked her over and over if she was all right, as if he couldn't hear her answer. Maybe he couldn't. Her voice hadn't been very strong.

To her relief, Adam had parked so that they couldn't see the scarred driver's side when they approached the car, and he opened the rear passenger door for her mother.

Cassie remained preoccupied until they got to the hotel. She got out when her mom did. "I'll walk to your room with you."

Mom smiled. "All right. Good night, Adam. I'm glad I got to know you a bit on this trip."

"Me too," Adam said. "Take your time, Cassie."

"He's very nice," Mom said once they were in the building.

"Yeah … I'm still getting to know him, but he does seem nice so far." Cassie pressed the elevator button.

"I wouldn't have been so worried about you if I knew you had that hunk looking out for you."

"Mom!" Cassie playfully swatted her mother's arm with her purse strap.

Mom giggled. "I really hope things go well for you. I'm praying for you."

Cassie hugged her mother goodbye at her door and wished her a safe trip. Then she tried to compose herself on her way back to the car.

Why did she have to call him a hunk? She sighed.

When she climbed in beside Adam, he put the engine in gear. "Your car seems to be running fine."

"Yeah, it was okay on the way home."

It had taken some finagling to get the vehicle back on the road after Schwam's driver rammed her, and she knew the deep dent and scrapes on the driver's side wouldn't be cheap to fix, but it hadn't acted or sounded weird on the way home.

"I'll take it to my mechanic in the morning and see what the worst is. They have a shuttle that can drop me off at work."

Adam nodded. "That's good. If you ever need a ride, you can call me."

"Thanks."

"I'm sure they can fix the dents and the paint job."

It seemed like a week had gone by since she left her apartment for work that morning. Cassie felt as if she were in a dream when Adam walked her to her door and handed her the car keys.

He looked down into her eyes. "Archie will understand if you don't come to work tomorrow."

He sounded as if he would say more, but Cassie cut him off. "No, I want things to be back to normal as quickly as possible. I think I'll quit being jumpy faster that way. But there is something you can do for me."

"All right."

"Come to Silver Dawn with me on Saturday. I'll be there on Friday of course, but I want to catch up with everyone when I have more time and make sure they're okay."

"I can do that."

"Thank you." Cassie looked up at him, suddenly nervous. Their only kiss so far had been brief and followed by the confrontation from Stevens. She hadn't really processed it.

Her anxiety was quickly put to rest when Adam pulled her into a hug instead. "I'm so glad you're safe."

She rested her head on his shoulder and let her breath out slowly. "It's over, right?"

"Yeah, it's over." He gave her a squeeze and let her go. "Stop in at the office before you go on your route tomorrow, all right?"

"I will."

He bent his head, and their lips met in a lingering kiss.

Cassie pulled away reluctantly, her pulse hammering.

"Good night."

He smiled. "See you tomorrow."

Cassie found Jenna waiting in her pajamas in the front room with teacups set out on the coffee table.

"All right," Jenna greeted her. "Go change, and then I want a full account of today."

Cassie smiled sheepishly and did as she was told.

Saturday finally came, and after dealing with slight tension for the last two days, Cassie had a sense of relief over the general normalcy of a day off. Adam picked her up around eleven in the morning, and they drove to Silver Dawn. Everyone came out to see them.

Lucy rushed to her and took Cassie's hand. "I just can't believe what those thugs put you through. You've been so brave. And you, too, Adam."

"Thank you." Cassie looked around at her elderly friends. No one was missing. "I guess no one's in the hoosegow so far."

"Nope," said Gerald. "We're in a little hot water, but the brass has been pretty understanding. I don't think any of us will do time."

"I'm so glad. I feel bad for Kieran, though."

Hal shook his head. "That boy has no common sense. Made things worse for himself by hiding the gun."

"Oh, we're not much better," said Ed. "Should have known better than to tamper with evidence."

Flossie pouted. "Well, how were we supposed to react to seeing a *body* on the walk? No one's prepared for that."

In contrast, Nita was smirking. "I just wish I had known why Kieran was acting so weird that day. Now we know he thought the body had just vanished on him. Oh, but Cassie, I want to show you something. Wait here." She scurried off toward her bungalow.

"So, Hal," Adam said.

Cassie turned back to Adam, who was looking pointedly at the woodworker.

Adam shifted his gaze downward. "Hal, I see you're holding Lucy's hand."

The other seniors, led by Ed, began whistling and catcalling.

Lucy blushed, but she smiled through it.

"So what?" Hal lifted her hand a little, as though he wanted to be sure no one missed it. "I like Lucy, and I'm not ashamed to say so."

Flossie clapped and Gerald joined in.

Cassie grinned. "That's great. Best wishes for you."

Nita emerged from her home and hustled back to the group. "See this?" she held out her hand to Cassie.

Cassie peered into the older woman's palm and saw a silver charm shaped like a garbage truck. "Oh, that's adorable!"

"I just got an order of them yesterday. I'm going to sell them in my shop. Inspired by you."

"I'm honored."

"And I put this one on a chain for you. Just be sure to tell folks where you got it." Nita winked.

"Absolutely. Thank you so much." Cassie took the silver chain and slipped it over her head. Lucy and Flossie stepped closer to examine it and nodded with approval.

Ed spoke up. "You know, Jeff's folks are saying they'll probably release his body soon. I want to go to the funeral, but only if I'm sure they don't know I was involved in … you know. Could be really awkward."

"We want to support the family, but we don't want to start a row at the funeral," Flossie explained.

Adam blew out a slow breath. "Yeah, I didn't think of that. I guess you could go, and then if anyone has a problem with your being there, just duck out as quietly as you can."

"We may do that," Ed said.

Adam could tell Cassie was in a better mood when he'd picked her up that morning. When they left Silver Dawn, she seemed even more cheerful. She must be relieved that her friends were doing well.

"It's after noon," he said. "Want to get lunch?"

"Sounds good. You pick. I'm okay with just about anything right now."

"All right. Hey, I have some news."

"Oh, yeah?"

"I've come up with a plan to start rehabilitating Boscoe. I'm going to ask the female volunteers to try smudging a little gun oil on their hands. Once he's used to the smell in safe situations, we can try introducing a prop gun while he's eating. If he can get calm around guns, I believe he can start letting men close to him again."

Cassie smiled at him. "Sounds like a solid plan." Her phone jingled, and she glanced at it. "That's Jenna."

"Go ahead and answer it."

Adam focused on driving, but he couldn't help hearing half of the conversation.

"Hi, what's up? … Oh. Mm-hmm … Wow … That makes sense. Yeah, I'm with Adam. I'll tell him."

Cassie's voice changed in tone. "Oh? What's that? Really? That's amazing! I'm so happy for you! Yes … absolutely. Yup, I'll see you later. Bye."

"More good news?" Adam asked.

"Travis proposed! And Jenna wants me to be a bridesmaid."

"Oh. That's cool. I'll have to congratulate them."

"Yeah. And before that, she said Travis told her a little bit about Stevens. Apparently the police here wanted someone to investigate Ollie Schwam undercover, but they didn't want it to be someone local cops would recognize. So, they installed Stevens in his gang months ago. Maybe even a year ago. He didn't help us the first time around because they had a big plan to take down the whole gang at once, and he couldn't blow his cover yet."

"Wow. I guess we almost messed up their plans."

"Jeff dying won't have helped either. I think he was pretty low-level, but not knowing who killed him probably put the whole mob on edge."

Adam nodded, thinking over the times he had seen Agent Stevens. Their cryptic encounter at the diner made a lot more sense now. Then his thoughts turned back to Jenna and Travis. "When will the wedding be?"

"She didn't say. They may not have decided yet."

Adam took a deep breath. "Is that what you want someday? To get married?"

Cassie appeared to squirm a little. Then she nodded. "Well, sure. I mean … someday."

Fighting a smile, Adam turned his truck into the parking lot of a restaurant chain. "I wonder who the lucky guy will be. Maybe if we keep getting to know each other, I'll find out."

She stared out the windshield. Her profile looked tense, and she fidgeted with her phone. He could barely hear her when she said, "Maybe so."

ABOUT PAGE M. DAVIS

Page M. Davis has published stories and compilations online. She also works as a kennel tech. She enjoys reading and drawing. A Maine native, she now lives with her rescue dog, Lisbon, south of the Mason-Dixon.

ABOUT SUSAN PAGE DAVIS

Susan Page Davis is the author of more than 100 novels. She has won numerous awards, including the Carol Award, three Will Rogers Medallions, and two Faith, Hope, and Love Readers' Choice Awards. A Maine native, she now lives in western Kentucky with her husband, Jim.

MYSTERIES BY SUSAN PAGE DAVIS

True Blue Mysteries

Blue Plate Special—**Book One**

https://scrivenings.link/blueplatespecial

Ice Cold Blue—**Book Two**

https://scrivenings.link/icecoldblue

Persian Blue Puzzle—Book Three

https://scrivenings.link/persianbluepuzzle

Scream Blue Murder—Book Four

https://scrivenings.link/screambluemurder

Scream Blue Murder—**Book Four**

https://scrivenings.link/truebluechristmas

Skirmish Cove Mysteries

Cliffhanger—**Book One**

https://scrivenings.link/cliffhanger

The Plot Thickens—Book Two

https://scrivenings.link/theplotthickens

Backstory—Book Three

https://scrivenings.link/backstory

Scrivenings
PRESS
Quench your thirst for story.
www.ScriveningsPress.com

Stay up-to-date on your favorite books and authors with our free e-newsletters.

ScriveningsPress.com

www.ingramcontent.com/pod-product-compliance
Lightning Source LLC
Chambersburg PA
CBHW070643100726
47907CB00007B/2087